HAWK

DEVIL'S MURDER MC

USA TODAY BESTSELLING AUTHOR

NIKKI LANDIS

Table of Contents

AUTHOR'S NOTE

Hawk is the third book in the Devil's Murder MC.

It's filled with dark and gritty content, a supernatural twist, steamy scenes, violence, biker slang, torture, kidnapping, and references to SA. Mature readers only. Heed the CWs and proceed with caution. Tough subjects occur in this book, please don't read if they will cause you discomfort.

I hope you enjoy Hawk and Callie's story.

The series contains ongoing storylines and themes that may not be resolved in every book, but each couple will eventually get their HEA.

COMMON TERMS

DMMC Devil's Murder Motorcycle Club. One-percenter outlaw MC with several chapters within the U.S. Founded in Henderson, NV 1981.

The Crow Shifter ability & shared soul of every Devil's Murder club member; a black feathered, predatory bird with enhanced traits.

Murder A group of crows, an omen of death.

Kraa An intense cry from a crow, fueled by strong emotion.

The Roost Bar & clubhouse owned by the Devil's Murder MC.

Bull's Saloon Second home to club members, bar owned by Lucky Lou.

Mobbing Individual crows assembling together to harass a rival or predator by cooperatively attacking it.

One-percenter Outlaw biker/club

Pres President of the club. His word is law.

Ol' lady A member's woman, protected wife status.

Cut Leather vest worn by club members, adorned with patches and club colors, sacred to members.

Church An official club meeting, led by president.

Chapel The location for church meetings in the clubhouse.

Prospect Probationary member sponsored by a ranking officer, banned from church until a full patch.

Full Patch A new member approved for membership.

Rook Former president, son of Jackdaw.

Crow Third generation club member, son of Rook, president.

Hog motorcycle

Cage vehicle

Muffler bunny Club girl, also called sweet butt, cut slut.

DDMC Dirty Death MC, rival motorcycle club.

HAWK
PLAYLIST

Crows – Saliva

Make Believe – Memphis May Fire

Punching Bag – Set It Off

Wait in the Truck – HARDY & Lainey Wilson

San Quentin – Nickelback

Welcome to My House – Nu Breed & Jesse Howard

Better Days – Cryptic Wisdom & Matty Beats

Black Vultures – Halestorm

Hometown Hurricane – Atlus

Unlive (with Yelawolf) – Jelly Roll

U Turn – Nu Breed & Jesse Howard

Son of a Sinner – Jelly Roll

You can find Nikki's Playlists on Spotify

HAWK

·:DEVIL'S MURDER MC:·

Hawk, Sergeant at Arms of the Devil's Murder MC, is loyal and cutthroat when it comes to his club. As a protector of his brothers, enforcer of the bylaws, and security, Hawk takes his position seriously, especially now that his president has been murdered by the Dirty Death MC. He won't rest until the blood of his enemies has been spilled, and justice served. He'll make damn sure that Rook is avenged and his son Crow doesn't meet the same fate.

But Hawk didn't count on the feisty, outspoken, desperate girl needing to rescue her sister from the dirty politician wreaking havoc in Nevada and the escort service that trafficked her out of the city. Callie is willing to do anything to bring her sibling home—even offer herself to a playboy biker who refuses to be shackled with an ol' lady.

Hawk never gave a damn about anything other than his club and brothers. Living free and wild without attachment kept his life simple and easy. Now, he's falling for this sweet girl and willing to invest in more than one night in his bed. Callie has him twisted up, ready to go to war to save her family and hoping to claim the innocent, curvy blonde he can't get out of his head. When she disappears, he knows he's the only one able to save her. Can Hawk protect her when everything comes crashing down, or will his need for vengeance risk both their lives?

ONE

HAWK

Five years ago—

"HEY, YOU GOOD TO ride, brother?"

"Shit. I'm dry as the fucking desert. I slept most of it off after Mara and Molly wore me out."

A loud guffaw followed my words as Rael slapped me on the back. "Shit, Hawk. You're welcome at the Crossroads anytime."

"Only if the twins keep me company again," I joked. Sort of. Those two blondes sucked me off and rode my dick until they drained me. Goddamn.

"Don't be a stranger. You need anything, man, hit me up."

"I will. See ya around, brother."

I swung my leg over my bike, dropping onto the seat.

I craved a smoke, but I needed to get on the road. Rook wanted me to return as soon as I finished up in Tonopah.

The ride to Henderson would take a few hours, and I was itchin' to get back to the Roost. Not that the RBMC hadn't shown me a good time. Shit. The Royal Bastards MC threw a hell of a party, and the rager was still going strong. Loud rock music blared from speakers inside the clubhouse, and the skunky smell of weed and cigarettes blended with sweat, leather, and whiskey. Damn tempting to stay another night. My cock twitched just thinkin' about it.

"Come back and kick it anytime, Hawk. We'll have a drink, smoke, whatever. Take your mind off shit for a bit."

That meant more than I could put into words. "Hell yeah."

The longstanding friendship between our clubs, specifically my pres Rook and Rael's pres Grim, had been close for years, birthed from mutual respect. Rook met Grim twenty years ago when he was a new member of the RBMC, and Rook became our pres, taking the reins from his father, Jackdaw. They formed a friendship that grew into a fierce brotherhood. The Crossroads welcomed our club like its own. A home away from home. Loyalty like that was a beautiful thing and it meant everything after the childhood I had.

My fist bumped the air as I rode outside the gates, merging onto Hwy 95. Moonlight shimmered on the asphalt surface as the miles disappeared beneath my tires, peeking behind wisps of fluffy gray clouds. The kind of moon that lit up the road surrounded by millions of twinkling stars. Best star gazing in Nevada.

Caw...caw.

My chin lifted, and I spotted the crow. His inky wings blotted the moon as he glided on a current of wind. He was never far behind me, watching, waiting, vigilant. Nothing was as loyal as the crow.

I had been riding for over two hours when I tensed, catching something on the road ahead. I felt weight drop on my left shoulder. A soft caw echoed close to my ear.

2

"I see it," I assured him, sensing his unease.

Alerted to possible danger, I knew I could reach my gun within a few seconds if the need arose. Never went anywhere without a weapon, usually with my hunting knife too. Felt naked without them and that included the cut I earned with every drop of sweat, busted knuckle, and bruised ego along the way.

People said the military broke you down, stripped you to the core, and then built you up again, teaching you to rely on your fellow soldiers, and push the boundaries of your physical limitations. Shit. They never prospected for a 1%er motorcycle club then. Child's play compared to what life as an outlaw entailed. Made me the man riding on this lonely stretch of Hwy 95 and heading through the dangerous desert without fear of man or beast. I'd seen hell in ways most folks didn't even have the courage to form nightmares about.

My headlights spotted an object on the highway. As I grew closer, I realized someone weaved unsteadily on their feet, crossing in and out of the median, stumbling once before regaining stability.

The crow flapped his wings. His round body bounced in agitation. He opened his beak and squawked as I rolled the throttle, squeezing in the clutch and downshifted, slowing my momentum to a crawl.

Caw...caw.

"I know. I see her."

Trying not to spook the woman on the road, I slowly pulled up next to her, blinking as I took in her appearance. A small muscle in my jaw ticked.

Shit from my past threatened to overtake my mind, knocking on that damn door I kept closed since my teen years.

Not fucking today. I shoved it away, concerned for the girl who fought for every inch of road she traveled.

The devil was the king of sinners and he sure enjoyed dragging others into the pit with him. I could see the handiwork of the motherfucker who bought into the devil's lies.

3

Tight jeans hugged the girl's ass and long legs, but that didn't snag my attention. It was her appearance. The athletic shoes on her feet were splattered with a dark substance. I'd been in enough fistfights to recognize drying blood.

As my gaze slid over the torn T-shirt she wore, stretched out at the neckline like someone had bunched the material in a fist, I clenched my teeth. And then I spotted bloodstains and several holes. *Fuck.*

A scrape on her bottom lip had split the skin open, revealing a gash next to a huge purple bruise on her jaw. Her left eye had swollen almost completely shut, surrounded by angry skin mottled red and purple. Her long brown hair ended in tangles, sticking up in odd places. Several scratches and additional bruising covered her bare arms.

I didn't doubt she'd been to hell and back again. She'd danced with the devil and lost.

One arm wrapped around her waist as she winced, shuffling her feet along the dirty asphalt. She didn't stop walking, staring straight ahead, focused on some unknown destination.

"Hey, honey," I greeted her, trying not to yell above the rumble of my engine.

Her head turned as she blinked, noticing me for the first time. I couldn't begin to imagine the demons she fought, choking on a sob she fought and failed to subdue. She almost collapsed before her body swayed, too overcome by trauma to function much longer.

She opened her mouth to speak, the truth hungering for exposure, but she didn't say a word.

The defeated expression on her face hit me hard, but it was the haunting sadness in her brown eyes that forced me to act. She carried a lifetime of sorrow on her shoulders and couldn't have been more than twenty-five. Years of being torn down had taken a toll and stolen her smile. No woman should endure and suffer as she did, broken and beaten by a man entrusted to protect and love her instead of using her as a punching bag.

4

I never could condone violence against women. Had my reasons why but it didn't change the facts.

The piece of shit that did this to her was gonna bleed for hurting her, and it fed the monster inside me to know that I would be the one setting him straight.

"Where is he?" The gruff tone of my voice must have spooked her because she startled, moving a strand of her hair out of her eyes with a shaky hand.

"Home."

"You'll show me." I didn't ask. Didn't need to know specifics. I sure as hell wasn't going to accept anything other than doling out a little of his own medicine to this asshole. "Hop on."

She blinked a few times before slowly climbing on behind me, holding onto the leather material of my cut like a lifeline. No, I didn't think ridin' on a Harley scared her, not after what she'd been through. It was probably adrenaline, shock, and pain from her injuries combined to wreak havoc on her body and emotions.

Over the next few minutes, she gave directions, leading me to a tan-colored double-wide mobile home in Indian Springs. A pickup truck was parked in the driveway with truck nuts. The plastic dangling scrotum was affixed to the bumper, sending a clear message. I snorted, not the least bit surprised this fucker suffered from small dick syndrome.

The bike slowly came to a stop as I rolled in front of the house. She didn't say a word, lifting her hand to point at the front door. Chipped green paint greeted me as I cut off the engine of my Harley and stood, placing the keys in her hand.

"If shit goes south, make sure my bike gets to the Devil's Murder MC. Rook will know what to do."

Her mouth popped open before she nodded. "Where do I find them?"

"You ever heard of Bull's Saloon?" I couldn't send her to the clubhouse. The location of the Roost wasn't public knowledge.

She blinked. "Yeah, I think so. The biker bar outside Vegas?"

"That's the one. Talk to Lucky Lou."

As I slipped on my brass knuckles, I ticked my chin in her direction. "Wait here. Stay with my bike."

She drew in a ragged breath, wincing from a wound I probably couldn't see. Beneath the bruises and scratches, she hid a slew of injuries and numerous scars. Years of abuse I couldn't begin to erase, even if I did prevent any further violence.

"Okay."

I didn't ask her any questions. There wasn't a need. The motherfucker that did this to her would learn not to place his hands on a woman in anger because I was breakin' every last one of his fingers to make sure that lesson hit home.

The front lawn was a bit overgrown as I walked toward the door, pounding my fist over the surface once I reached it. No one answered, and there wasn't a sound to prove anyone was home. I knew better.

Annoyed, I lifted my foot and kicked it in, watching with satisfaction as the wood splintered and the frame cracked. I stomped over the threshold with one purpose my sole focus—retribution—a reckoning.

The devil's reject was comin' to exact a little justice.

If only I could have done that for my mom.

"What the fuck!?"

I didn't pause as the man on the living room couch stumbled to his feet, knocking over a couple of beer bottles as they crashed to the floor and shattered into dozens of tiny pieces. He didn't notice the glass slicing into his feet as he slurred, threatening me for entering his house. I snarled when I noticed the blood on his swollen knuckles.

In the corner, I spotted a 12-gauge and knew I couldn't let him get close enough to use it.

6

I'd studied Brazilian jiu-jitsu after my old man used to knock me around as a kid. The self-defense martial art and combat sport based on grappling, ground fighting, and submission holds had grown from a necessity to a passion. I loved the flexibility and burn of my muscles, the flood of adrenaline when I pushed my body to the limit. I stopped being a punching bag the day I stood up to my father and blocked the hit aiming for my head, shocking the hell out of him.

To this day, I never let a man get the best of me or gain the advantage. I learned to watch my opponents and anticipate their moves. That skill proved useful when I patched into the Devil's Murder. I earned my place in the club with blood, sweat, and loyalty and never looked back.

So when I saw this motherfucker move toward his weapon, I never had to think about what to do next. My body moved without conscious thought.

I let the hammer drop.

Lunging in his direction, I lifted his leg, knocking the abusive fucker off balance. He crashed to the ground, groaning as I swung my fist. The brass knuckles I wore grazed the left side of his face as his head bounced off the carpet. I swung a few more times, enjoying the splatter of blood and his swelling face. Motherfucker deserved a hell of a lot worse.

I whipped my gun free, pointing the barrel at his forehead. "We're gonna get something straight, asshole. You lift a finger to hurt another woman, and I'll be back." I pointed to the patches on my cut. "You see these?"

He squinted, nodding as he read the Devil's Murder MC logo.

"I'll return with my entire club. Trust me when I say they won't find anything left of you to bury. I know everywhere in the fuckin' desert to scatter your pathetic ass for the crows to feast."

"Fuck," he spit, turning his head while he groaned. "That bitch isn't worth it."

His remark pissed me off.

7

"You don't ever lift a finger to hurt a woman again. Got it?"

His hand rose, and he flipped me off. "Fuck you."

Really? This guy was dumber than I thought. Did he think I was messin' around?

His attitude needed an adjustment. I called to the crow, grinning wide when I heard him rush inside the house through the open front door, flapping his wings and scolding the bloodied man on the ground.

"I guess this lesson is gonna be learned the hard way."

I stomped on his right hand, feeling several of his bones snap. He screamed as I pistol-whipped the side of his head, watching with satisfaction as his eyes rolled back.

"Lights out, bitch."

Yanking my knife out of my cut, I bent down, carving *wife beater* into his forehead. With any luck, it would leave a scar.

Caw...caw.

"Yeah. Yeah. You're getting your turn. Take his eye."

Backing away, I stared down at the bloody message forever etched into this prick's skin. Maybe that would stop his abuse.

The crow hopped on his chest, quivering with excitement. His beady eyes blinked before his head tilted to the side. Another caw escaped.

"No. Only one eye. Don't kill him."

The crow protested, hopping around as he berated me for denying him justice.

"Hey. We've been over this. We don't kill unless it's necessary."

The crow's puffed chest deflated. He turned around, shaking out his onyx feathers.

"Just the one eye," I reminded him.

All I got in response was a short, exasperated caw.

Fucking cranky ass bird.

I dropped to the floor, picked up the limp left hand, and snapped the rest of this asshole's fingers.

There. A matching set.

"Have fun wiping your ass, you abusive fuck."

The crow tittered, perching on the man's nose. He stared me down.

"Okay. Fine. I'll leave you to peck his eye in peace."

Damn.

Mumbling about the crow's ridiculous need to feast without an audience, I stomped outside, pausing to pick up a pack of smokes off the end table. I ignored the blood staining my fingers and plucked out a cigarette, lighting up as I sat on a chair. The tiny porch didn't have much furniture, but I managed to plant my boots on the worn metal table, waiting for the cops to show up. Made me smile as I inhaled to know I stole them from the man inside.

"Is he dead?"

The young woman watched me smoke an entire cigarette before speaking, her gaze falling on the bloodied brass knuckles I slipped off, wiping on my jeans before slipping into a pocket.

"Nope. Bet he wishes he was once he wakes up, though."

She chewed her bottom lip. "Why?"

"Let's just say an eye for an eye."

She sank onto an empty chair across from me. "Jed didn't start out hitting me."

"Doesn't matter, honey."

"I guess not."

"Anyone you want to call?" I asked, smacking the pack into my palm before sliding out another of the Marlboro Reds. Picking up my lighter, I lit the end, drawing the nicotine into my lungs.

"My sister Callie."

"I reckon you don't have a phone."

She shook her head. "Too much money."

"Bet he spent whatever he wanted." Asshole. "Here." I swiped across my cell as I pulled it from my cut. "Call your sister. Tell her where to find you."

She didn't hesitate to reach for the device, tapping in her sister's number. I heard it ring twice before a sexy as fuck female voice answered.

"Hello?"

"Callie, it's me."

"Sadie!? Are you okay?"

"No, but I think I will be," she managed to say before the tears began to fall.

I stood up, giving her a little privacy as I watched the road for red and blue lights. Once I had my phone call, I'd let Rook and the club know where I got locked up. Not much point in contacting my pres until then. Wasn't shit they could do.

"So, Sadie," I began, accepting my cell as she handed it over. "I can call you Sadie, right?"

"I think you earned the right," she joked, wincing when the half smile on her lips tugged at the cut and bruising beginning to form around her mouth.

"Tell me you won't be a man's punching bag again."

"No." She touched the side of her swollen face. "That's why I left him." She stared at me with big brown, curious eyes, even if one of them couldn't open more than a slit.

Nodding, I realized that was why I found her on the road. "My old man liked to solve problems with his fist," I admitted, answering her unspoken question, "when I was strong and big enough, I learned to become better at it than he did."

She swallowed hard. "You hit him back?"

"Only took one night to set him straight," I mused aloud, taking a long hit from the cigarette. "He spent three months in rehab and never could walk right again after I busted his knees and ankles with a bat. Didn't hurt my mamma again until I moved out."

"Oh shit."

"Yeah. He got to her one night when I was out of town." Fuck. I didn't want to think about that night.

"She's gone?" Her eyes filled with tears, not for what she endured, but because of my loss.

"I couldn't save her," I choked, hating the memory.

Sadie's breath sawed in and out of her chest as she shook her head. "I'm sorry."

What a sweetheart. She deserved better than the life she'd known.

"I got justice," I replied with finality. And that was the cold, hard truth. The reason I didn't care if I spent time behind bars. I did it once to save a woman's life and it seemed like a damn good reason to repeat the experience. My mother survived another ten years on this earth before the man who fathered me ended her life. At least I could say he didn't breathe for long afterward.

Something in me closed off and hardened when I lost my mom. I shut off my emotions after burying her. To this day, I kept my heart guarded. Didn't believe in love or romance. Maybe someday I would meet the woman who made that statement a lie.

Sadie swallowed, placing her hand over mine. "Thank you for getting justice for me too."

"You're welcome, honey."

She withdrew her hand, sliding it across the table and onto her lap. "Is Hawk your real name? Or just the one you use?" Her gaze swept over my cut, reading the patches.

"It's my road name."

"Okay. A pleasure to meet you, Hawk."

Smirking, I nodded. "You ain't lyin'."

We didn't say much else, sitting in the warm night air until the cops finally arrived. Cuffed and placed in the back of a cruiser, I ticked my head her way. "Don't forget about my bike."

"I won't. I'll make sure it gets to your club."

Satisfied, I rested back against the seat.

Caw...caw.

The crow landed a few feet away, swaying his head from side to side before shaking out his feathers.

"I know."

Gonna be a long while before I set foot outside as a free man again.

TWO

HAWK

One year earlier—

"So, YOU'RE GETTIN' OUT Friday," Sadie began, twirling a long lock of her dark hair around her finger. "That's good."

"Sure is, honey. Lookin' forward to ridin' home and far from this hellhole."

One of the guards snorted behind me and I laughed. I learned quickly how to stay out of trouble and play the game while on the inside. Life within these walls had its own set of rules.

Sitting back against my chair, I took in Sadie's appearance. She seemed like she had something on her mind.

I'd seen her enough over the last three years to tell when she felt anxious. Her restlessness coincided with mine but for entirely different reasons. I couldn't wait to set foot outside these prison walls again and escape the dark void that had pulled me under since my incarceration.

Sadie had demons I couldn't begin to fathom and none of them had anything to do with the reason we both sat here today.

I got pinched. It was my choice and I stood by it. I wasn't a fucking pussy. I could own my shit.

There wasn't more to say.

But Sadie? Did she deal with the abuse and move on? I couldn't say for sure.

"How's the sessions going?"

She finally took my advice after the nightmares became too much and began seeing a therapist.

"Good. Really good, Hawk. I'm learning a lot about myself and how to maintain boundaries. It's not easy, but I'm dealing with all the trauma." She shrugged, a smile forming on her lips. "I met someone. He's sweet, patient, and didn't run when he heard about my past."

"That's fucking amazing." I meant that.

She pushed her hair over her shoulders, clearing her throat. I could sense she had something she needed to get off her chest. The wounds from that night had faded long ago but they left behind physical scars. One by her mouth and another by her eyebrow. A reminder of her strength and perseverance.

I searched her eyes, staring at the beautiful face of a survivor. Over the last three years, she'd gained confidence and reclaimed the parts of herself she lost.

A gorgeous girl inside and out, she made me feel special just by showing up twice a month to check in. Had the circumstances been different I probably would have been attracted to and flirted with Sadie. Hell, I would've taken her on a ride on my Harley and my cock, but I didn't see her like that. Couldn't. Not after the way we met.

"You think you'll find happiness?"

Ah. Now I understood why she seemed a little solemn today.

14

"Don't doubt it. All I need is my bike and the open road to find a little peace." I meant that. I learned a long time ago to let the past go and not dwell on it.

"That sounds too easy."

"Babe, life is only as hard as you make it. I live for the simple things like beer, my club, and pussy."

The corners of her lips lifted in a little smile before faltering. "Being here didn't make you bitter?"

"You askin' if I regret what I did that night? Fuck no. Any bitterness I got inside ain't from you."

Her shoulders relaxed. "Good to know, Hawk."

Glad we had that settled.

"I guess you'll be returning to your life in the club. Motorcycles and mayhem. Right?"

I couldn't help laughing at her description. "Yeah. Been missin' my bike."

Caw...caw.

And the crow too. He never strayed far from the prison. Even now, I could feel his presence, restless for my release.

The Class C felony I'd been charged with held a maximum five-year sentence and the judge shackled me with it, pissed I'd broken into a man's home and assaulted him. Didn't seem to be fazed by the fact he beat on his girlfriend. Sadie testified but it didn't matter. In the judge's eyes I was a thug who already had a criminal history. He didn't seem to like my affiliation with a 1%er biker club.

He tried hard as hell to blame me for the crow pecking out Jed's eye, but there wasn't any proof.

I made friends during my stint and didn't fuck up by doing anything stupid. After serving three of the five years, I was informed by the parole board that I was a free man at the end of this month.

Staring across the table at Sadie, I didn't regret my choices. It was worth it to see the young woman who had been so broken and bloody that night regain her confidence and the freedom to live life any way she wanted.

We only talked about Jed once when she discovered he had lost his eye and all his fingers had been broken. I admitted I carved a message onto his forehead with my knife. Felt damn good when I learned the skin scarred as I had hoped.

"I hope you won't be a stranger once you're out but maybe that's weird."

Frowning, I wasn't sure what she meant. "Gotta be straight with me, honey. Mixed messages aren't my thing."

"I'd like to keep in touch. Even if we just text or call once in a while. No commitment," she laughed at my expression. "You'll always be someone I care about, Hawk. I need to know you're out there, riding your bike, and enjoying your freedom."

I could do that. "Sure, Sadie. I'd like that."

Four days later, I walked outside the gates, breathing in the fresh air untainted by the shackles I'd worn for three long years. A few of my club brothers stood by a row of Harleys, ready to greet me. Crow, Cuckoo, and Talon had shown up often over the last thirty-six months. Their visits kept me going.

Matching grins spread across their faces as I ticked my chin in greeting.

"Shit. If it ain't our SAA, joining society again, all reformed and respectable."

Snorting, I shook my head. "I don't think those are the words I'd use, Crow."

He laughed, pulling me in for a hug. "Missed you, brother."

"Yeah, I missed you all too," I announced, slapping him on the back as I stepped away, turning to Cuckoo. "The fuck happened to you?"

Cuckoo shrugged. "I don't know what you mean."

"You look like a fucked up version of the Easter Bunny. That's some sick shit."

Cuckoo snickered.

He wore a white Easter bunny suit with the hands and feet cut off, black leather gloves, and boots in their place. Fake blood splattered the pink chest. His cut draped over the ensemble.

He was into some weird shit, including a fascination with anything horror themed. I didn't want to think about last Halloween.

Cuckoo wore a deranged bunny head with long pointy ears. One had been ripped in half; the other slashed in a few places with a knife. Same with one of the pink cheeks. Fake blood droplets spattered the sharp teeth in the gaping mouth. His face peaked through as he sucked on a giant green lollipop.

I swear to fuck, that kinky fucker wasn't entirely right in the head.

"Why the fuck do we let you out in public?"

Talon shoved Cuckoo. "He's pretty, that's why."

I shook my head, striding over to my bike. All I needed was to ride. My hand glided over the chrome and sleek black paint.

"I missed you, baby."

Two minutes later, we merged onto the highway.

Bright Nevada sunshine glared down from above as the scorching heat wrapped my body in a sweltering embrace. The steady thrum of my bike's engine rumbled beneath me as I turned my head to the side, catching the black shadow on the ground, soaring high above, casting the crow's wings on the dusty ground as he spread them wide.

Even incarcerated, I felt his presence. The crow never left me.

He might have been separated, but I caught his flight every afternoon, cawing as he dropped onto the windowsill of the library. He hopped from window to window, giving me an earful. Admonished by a fucking bird with black wings.

But that was all behind me now.

For the first time, I felt free. That was too fucking amazing to dwell on anything else.

THREE

CALLIE

Five months ago—

"I NEED TO TALK to you," Sadie announced as I answered her incoming call, annoyed as I noted the time was nearly eleven p.m., and I just finished a grueling shift at work. Waitressing wasn't what I wanted to do for the rest of my life, but it paid the bills while I found a real job and began my career. I'd earned a business degree and graduated over three months ago, but I still hadn't found a job in my field.

"It's late, Sadie. What's going on?"

I should have been more patient. Tired and rubbing my aching feet as I collapsed against the mattress in my bedroom, I stifled a groan. I needed a shower and sleep.

"Hey, it's important. Seriously."

She said that every time we spoke. Always a new gig or drama or bullshit.

If my older sister wasn't such a mess, I wouldn't be hesitating. Only two years and five days separated us.

Sometimes I felt decades older. As the responsible sister, I always kept my nose clean and avoided breaking the rules. Never had a speeding ticket or paid my rent late. I worked my ass off to be a good citizen and make my parents proud.

Sadie had been picked up for everything from prostitution to petty theft. She was a bit of a kleptomaniac and enjoyed being the life of the party. I didn't think there was a single drug out there she hadn't tried, although I knew she enjoyed ecstasy the most. Far too impulsive, she rarely thought through the consequences of her actions until it was too late.

None of this changed the fact that I loved my sister. She had a good heart and believed the best in people until they proved otherwise. She was a glass-half-full kind of personality. Driven by an unforeseen motor, she was always on the go. Sadie was diagnosed with attention deficit hyperactivity disorder, or ADHD at age seven. She'd been medicated for it since, but I doubted she regularly remembered to take the pills she needed.

"Could we talk tomorrow?" I stifled a yawn, resisting the urge to close my eyes. That shower wasn't happening until morning now because I wouldn't have any energy left once my conversation with Sadie ended.

"Callie."

Her desperate, worried tone caught my attention, and I sat up. "Tell me what's happening."

"I-I think someone is trying to," she paused and swallowed loudly, "kill me."

"Shit."

"Exactly."

"Come over right now. I'll put on a pot of coffee."

"I'm already outside your door. Open up!"

Scrambling to my feet, I held onto the phone as I sprinted into the hallway, down the stairs, and to the back door of my townhome.

Flinging open the door, I found my sister shivering and soaked from the heavy downpour outside.

Pulling her in, I slammed the door shut behind her and flipped every lock. "Jesus. Get undressed. I'll bring you some dry clothes."

Sadie's slim figure shivered as she peeled off her black cocktail dress. The material clung to every inch of her body, molding her hourglass figure. She had legs a mile long and kicked off her strappy four-inch heels, ringing out the wet strands of her hair over the kitchen sink as I returned with a towel, oversized t-shirt, black leggings, and warm socks.

In true Sadie style, she stripped without a single glance in my direction. She'd never been ashamed of her body or being naked, which hadn't changed over the years. If anything, she grew bolder. That could explain her current profession—professional escort.

Of course, if I had her figure, I'd flaunt it too. Sadie took after our father's side of the family. Tall, slender, athletic, and perfectly flawless skin that always looked kissed by the sun. Me? I followed after our mother—fuller hips and thighs, round ass, and bigger breasts. I didn't hate my body by any means, but I sometimes wished I had her toned, flat stomach and height.

Wistfully, I set to work brewing a pot of strong coffee. The past had proved nights like this with Sadie would be lengthy. I needed the caffeine, or I'd fall asleep upright in my chair.

"Tell me you have Cinnabon creamer." Her long dark hair hung in loose waves over her shoulders as I turned, ticking my chin at the fridge.

"Of course. I'm not a Neanderthal."

Sadie snorted, whipping open the fridge. She pulled out the container of Cinnabon creamer and popped open the top.

Inhaling, she smiled. "Smells just like a fresh cinnamon roll with cream cheese icing."

"Our favorite," I agreed.

After passing a mug her way, I filled mine most of the way with coffee, adding enough creamer to change the color.

Sadie had already poured a generous amount of the creamer into her cup, nearly filling the mug halfway before adding coffee. Some things never changed. I couldn't help snickering at the obscene amount of the Cinnabon concoction she used.

Years ago, when we used to live together and both attended college, we'd wake up every morning like this and share a pot before classes began. That was before she dropped out to pursue her acting career, as short-lived as it was.

My sister sat beside me in one of the four wooden chairs surrounding my tiny square dining room table. We both sipped on the coffee, gaining the boost we'd need for the heavy conversation I knew would be difficult to hear.

"Remember when we used to do this every morning?"

"I was just thinking about it," I admitted, giving her a warm smile. "Some of my best memories. Just the two of us."

"Yeah. Good times." Her smile faltered a little. "I'm sorry I didn't stick around."

"Hey, I know. You don't have to apologize."

"But I want to, sis. You know staying in one place too long isn't easy for me. I get antsy."

"I think that's putting it mildly," I agreed.

She smirked at that comment. "The thing is, I tend to get lost sometimes." She paused, staring at my kitchen with a frown. "When did you paint the walls this lemon-yellow color?"

Perfect example.

"Six months ago."

"Damn. I guess I didn't notice."

She did on her last visit but didn't remember.

"Well, it's not important."

Sadie shook her head. "No, it's not." She sighed softly, lifting her head to meet my curious gaze. "Do you remember when I told you I had a lot of important customers as my clientele?"

"At the DOLL Agency?" One of the more discreet escort companies in the Las Vegas area, the DOLL Agency offered companions to wealthy, high-profile clients. Men like politicians and CEOs of Fortune 500 companies who relished showing up to events and ritzy clubs with beautiful women on their arms.

I hated that my sister chose this profession because I knew for a fact that these men wanted more than a pretty face by their side for a few hours in public. These men had specific sexual appetites and solicited sex even if it was illegal. The thing was, prostitution was legal in ten of Nevada's seventeen counties. They could pick up women whenever they wanted, but these men wanted the model-perfect figures and dazzling beauties the DOLL Agency boasted among their employees.

My sister was a glorified prostitute, but she didn't see it that way. Sadie had more money in the bank than anyone I knew. The perks of her job were obvious—an expensive apartment in a secure building overlooking the city lights in Las Vegas with clear panes of glass exposing every breathtaking detail, more diamonds and jewelry than a Tiffany & Co retailer, a bright blue Corvette, and the luxury to sleep in every day, stopping for a manicure, pedicure, and any other spa service she wanted any day of the week.

Even with all those amenities, I couldn't sleep with a man I didn't have a connection with and felt some affection for. It wasn't in my nature. Maybe Sadie could separate herself from that part of the business easier than I could. As far as I knew, she'd been an escort for three years and loved it.

"I sent you some money."

Narrowing my eyes, I shook my head. "Sadie," I began.

"I know what you're gonna say. You always say the same thing. Doesn't matter. I need you to take it."

"Why?" I asked, suspicious of her innocent expression.

"So I know you're taken care of. Don't fight me on this. It's already in your PayPal account. Refuse it, and I'll keep sending you more."

Ugh. "I'm not a charity case, Sadie."

"No. You're my sister, and I want to know that you're okay when I'm not around. You don't have enough food in your pantry or fridge."

What did she do? Scope it out when I wasn't paying attention?

I picked up my phone, opened my PayPal account, and gasped when I saw the amount. My sister had sent me twenty-five thousand dollars. What. The. Hell.

"I can't accept this."

"You will," she replied firmly. "Pay off that car and stop stressing about your rent. Now you've got time to find a job you want instead of waitressing and relying on tips to get by."

Shit. I bit my lip, trying not to cry. "Sadie. This is too much."

"It's nothing to me. I want you to take it. It'll give you a whole year to figure out what you want to do and find the right job for your career."

She was right. Eighteen thousand would pay my rent for a year, and another three would pay off my car. That left four for food and utilities, and that's if I stopped working or didn't do anything else on the side.

"You're going to make me cry," I finally blurted, blinking as a few tears escaped. "Thank you."

She reached over and hugged me. "You worked your ass off for that degree. I want you to be happy, Callie. You deserve it."

Hugging her back, I squeezed a little too tight. "I love you, sis."

"Love you too, more than anything."

I leaned back, swiping under my eyes to get rid of the tears. "So, tell me what's going on."

Sadie held the mug in two hands, taking a long sip before she set the cup down. "Mayor Elliot Goodman has become one of my regular clients, and he's . . . clingy."

Blink. Blink. "The Henderson Mayor? Like where we live?"

"Yes." She snorted at my response. "Clingy probably isn't the right word." She bit her lip, staring off into space for a few seconds. "Obsessed is more accurate."

"That sounds dangerous," I observed.

"You have no idea." She finished her coffee and rose, refilling the mug and adding more Cinnabon creamer. "He's manipulative and demanding, pushing me to drop my other clients. He wants a personal escort at his beck and call, ready to fuck him or do his bidding any moment of the day."

"Screw that!" I exclaimed, pushing my mug aside. "Tell me you didn't agree to it."

"Of course not."

"Okay. Good."

"But he's not taking it well," she replied carefully.

"What does that mean? You said you think someone is trying to kill you. Who? The freaking mayor?"

She swallowed hard. "I haven't been truthful with you, not for a long time. Three years, to be exact."

Frowning, I had no idea what she meant. "What are you telling me?"

"I'm not really an escort. Never have been, sis."

Confused, I didn't know what to say.

"I've been undercover all this time."

"Undercover?" What the hell did that mean?

"I got picked up for soliciting and prostitution three years ago when I was first hired as an escort. The feds were trying to shut down an international trafficking ring and knew the DOLL Agency was intimately connected."

"Wow," I whispered, shocked. "You never said a word."

How could she keep a secret like that and not tell me?

"I couldn't," she confided, her expression pained. "I took the deal they offered. Since then, I've been helping to gather evidence against the DOLL Agency, its clientele, and now, the mayor. I can't cut ties with him. It's part of the case they're building."

"Shit," I cursed, understanding how complicated the situation had become for my sister. "Why are you telling me this now?"

"Because, as I said, I think someone is trying to kill me for the knowledge I've gained. I'm not sure, but they must have figured out I'm the mole."

Oh no. "Jesus, Sadie."

"Yeah, it's as bad as you're imagining. I don't think the feds can protect me. I've gotten too involved and learned too much."

"But your life is in danger. That has to mean it's time to pull you out. Right?"

"It's not that simple. They still need to finish building their case. If I leave, I take the chance away from prosecuting these men for the crimes they've committed. I've lost friends. Good people." Her voice broke, and Sadie cleared her throat. "I won't let their disappearances and deaths mean nothing."

The missing girls in Nevada from the news. It all clicked now. I'd seen the reports for months on the local stations. Over a dozen women missing in the last eighteen months. Sadie must have known some of them.

I reached for my sister's hand, folding my fingers around her cool skin. "I don't want you to risk your life. You're someone important too."

She tried to smile and failed. "I love you, Callie. Don't doubt it, but I could never live with myself if I didn't see this through to the end."

The finality of those words terrified me. "Sadie. If it gets too hot, you get out. I don't care how. Contact me, and I'll find you."

A soft sigh left her lips. "I don't know if that's possible."

"But if it is, promise me you'll try."

"Okay." She squeezed my hand. "There's an agent that I trust. He's become a close friend—someone trying to help and protect me. I had to memorize his information since I couldn't keep his name or number in my phone. Give me your cell, sis."

I released her hand, sliding it across the table.

Sadie unlocked the device, already knowing my password. I guess I was a little predictable. Couldn't remember the last time I updated or changed any of my passwords. She typed in the info and handed it back. "Agent Carson Phillips is trustworthy. He knows how to get in contact with me if anything comes up."

"Is he your handler or something?"

"Or something."

Sadie blushed, and I sat back, staring at her with surprise.

"You like him."

A slow smile spread across her face. "Carson is unlike anyone I've ever met. He's sweet and charming but also brutally honest and doesn't mess around. He's strict and always follows the rules. Well, except for that one time," she trailed off, fidgeting in her seat. "Yeah. Just once."

The dreamy look on her face and how she described Agent Phillips proved she'd developed feeling for the guy.

"Be careful. Please. I don't want you hurt when this is over."

"I," she began, shaking her head, "I'm a realist, sis. I know nothing can work between us, but it doesn't stop me from wishing things were different. I believe, I *know*, Carson cares about me. He keeps things professional because there's no other choice. Both of us must be careful."

"But the heart wants what it wants," I mused aloud.

"It's scary how well you understand me," she joked.

"So, to be clear, it's not just the mayor we need to worry about. These traffickers are a problem."

Sadie nodded. "Yes. And their business associates, including a motorcycle club, called the Dirty Death."

"That's ominous."

"Isn't it?" She wasn't listening to me fully, lost in her thoughts. Not that I could blame her. This had nothing to do with her ADHD. My sister fought the overwhelming, devastating truth that awaited when she left and returned to the fate that awaited her outside these sheltered walls.

"You stay as far away from them as you can."

She blinked, staring into my eyes with a resolution that completely freaked me out. "I already met the president of the club, Undertaker. He likes having me around."

I stood up so fast I almost knocked my chair over. My heart was jackhammering inside my chest. Worry and fear for my sister took hold. What would happen to Sadie once the feds got what they needed? How the hell did she get away unharmed and live a normal life?

Sadie had been through so much. Before her job at the escort service, she'd been in the hospital for multiple injuries as the result of her asshole boyfriend who abused her. He'd finally gone to prison thanks to a biker who kicked his ass and helped Sadie escape. Hawk, if I remembered the name right, nearly killed her ex. It wouldn't have been a loss. Jed deserved what happened to him. That was five years ago, and I hated that my sister only escaped one tough, life-threatening situation to be placed in another. It wasn't fair.

I threw my arms around her, trembling with the realization that I could lose my sister because of this deal she made. I wished she'd gone to jail instead. At least she wouldn't be risking her life with human traffickers, a deadly motorcycle club, and a corrupt politician.

Was that naïve? Probably.

Sadie calmly brushed her hand down my hair, returning my hug. Her voice was far steadier than it should have been. "It's going to work out. You'll see."

I didn't share her confidence.

FOUR

CALLIE

One month earlier—

SADIE DISAPPEARED. MY WORST fear had come to pass. I didn't know what happened, but I wasn't getting any answers from the police. I filed a report and had her declared officially missing, but no one seemed to be doing anything about it. At least, no one else besides Agent Phillips.

We discussed that when he called to check-in. His tone betrayed his frustration at the lack of new leads on her case.

"You haven't told anyone about me, right?"

He asked every time we spoke. "No. I'm not stupid. Revealing my connection to you would ruin everything."

"Yeah, okay. Just making sure, Callie." He sighed. "I don't like this. She's never failed to check-in. We've been working on this case for almost three years. Sadie always comes through no matter what. I don't like it."

I never told him what my sister confided about their feelings for one another, and he'd kept that information to himself. Maybe he didn't want his superiors to find out since that could jeopardize all the hard work everyone had put in over the last thirty-six months.

I didn't blame Agent Phillips for keeping his secrets, but it only increased my anxiety. "What's happening with the case?"

"I've got some interviews today and a few things to follow up on."

I was tired of his vague answers. He didn't owe me shit, but he did owe it to Sadie. She risked her life for the FBI and the intel they wanted. "And that means?"

"Callie. I'm doing everything I can—"

"That's not good enough. Maybe we need to go back to her apartment. We could have missed something."

"I've been there multiple times. Nothing new—"

"Agent Phillips!" My patience, along with my manners, had run off, likely never to come back. "This is my sister. My blood. She's my family. You don't understand—"

"I do, Callie," he interrupted harshly. "I care about Sadie more than I can reveal. She's, I," he stumbled, his voice cracking, "I love her," he revealed, his tone lowering to a whisper. "You need to know I won't stop searching for her. I swear it."

Sighing, I knew I should ease up on him a little. "She's the most important person in my world. You understand?"

"Yeah," he replied softly," because she's *mine* too."

I guess we were on the same page then. "Okay. I trust you. Don't give up, and don't fail. You need to find her and bring Sadie home."

"I will," he swore.

I ended the call, pacing the hardwood floors of my apartment as I had been doing for the last month since my sister disappeared.

Since the night she came to me and confessed the truth, I'd been uneasy, terrified that the police would show up at my door and ask me to identify her body. I chewed all my nails down too. The lack of answers and stress took a toll.

I had to do something. Idleness wasn't helping.

That was how I ended up working at Mayor Elliot Goodman's office. The part-time secretarial position appeared online as a new job opening, and I filled out an application, interviewed, and was hired that same week, working for that chauvinist, creepy sexual predator. The mayor ogled me like a juicy steak the entire interview, and if I didn't have to pretend indifference because of my sister, I would have walked out.

He must have been too preoccupied because I shared the same last name as my sister, and he didn't seem to notice. Weeks later, I avoided Elliot as much as possible. The plan to learn new information about Sadie's disappearance was a disaster until I met Bree. Brianna Hart became a trusted friend when I finally admitted why I applied for the job.

She sat across from me in the break room, sipping coffee as I clenched my hands. Anxious, I didn't know what to say since I couldn't reveal my association with Agent Phillips. Sure, I said he was working the case, but I didn't elaborate on the connection we shared or how close he'd gotten to Sadie.

"You can trust me, Callie. I don't have any love for the mayor. He's despicable."

"You don't know all the things he's done," I spat. "The women he's hurt."

"You're wrong," she contradicted, lowering her voice. "I've seen emails and correspondence. I've heard Elliot on the phone. He doesn't hide anything. I know about the escort service."

My gaze snapped to her green eyes, afraid of what she'd piece together. If Bree connected the dots, it was only a matter of time before the mayor did too.

Shit.

I decided to lay it out for her and hoped she'd help me. If not, I wouldn't be returning to this job tomorrow. I couldn't risk anything happening to my sister as a result of my reckless idea to work here.

"My sister is missing. She's an escort for the DOLL Agency. I know Elliot Goodman solicited her services. He picked her up on a date the night she disappeared."

Brianna blinked, sitting back in her chair. "You're here to find out what happened."

"Yes. I won't let this go. I need to locate Sadie and bring her home." Clearing my throat, I fought back tears. "The mayor can't figure out why I'm here or my connection to my sister."

"He's not going to find out, Callie. I promise." She reached across the table, placing her hand over mine. "I'll help any way that I can."

"Good. I'm going to need it."

OVER THE NEXT FEW weeks, Bree began digging into the mayor's files. She didn't find the smoking gun we hoped for, but she did begin to compile evidence against him. Letters, emails, contracts, and other correspondence that proved Elliot's misappropriation of funds and criminal activity. She used a flash drive to download what documents she could from her computer, but we both knew she'd have to sneak into Elliot's office and access the data he kept there soon.

Elliot had a business meeting this evening, and Bree planned to log onto his desktop and obtain all the info she could once he left. The day seemed to drag on while we waited.

"Is he using the same escort service again?"

"Yeah, and he's sloppy about it. Doesn't even hide the information from me. He had me call the DOLL Agency and double-check that his favorite girl was ready for tonight." She shook her head and sighed. "He sent her the same package as Sadie."

I swallowed audibly, hating the confirmation. "Two dozen red roses tied with a black ribbon, a black cocktail dress, and instructions."

"Yes," Bree confirmed. "I saw the receipts today. He didn't bother hiding them."

"He thinks he's untouchable," I spat, pissed he planned to use another girl the same way he did with my sister.

The night Sadie disappeared, the mayor requested her services from the DOLL Agency and sent the package. It couldn't be a coincidence. My sister sent me a text describing the roses, cocktail dress, and the note he'd left her. She told me to stay safe and vigilant. If she hadn't contacted me the next day, I needed to call Agent Phillips.

I never ended up making the call. He dialed my number early in the morning, worried when Sadie never showed up at their rendezvous point. No one had heard from her since midnight, long before her check-in with Agent Phillips. I refused to believe she died. In my heart, I felt my sister was alive and needed our help. No way in hell would I give up trying to find and bring her back home.

"What's the plan?" I asked Bree, unable to sit still. "It's taking too long to find Sadie. It's been weeks since she went missing. I'm worried."

"Stay calm. We have to keep up appearances."

Ugh. I hated that she was right.

"Go back to your desk. When Elliot leaves for the meeting, I'll text you."

Sighing, I stood, leaving the break room to resume my monotonous secretarial duties. The job was meaningless, the tasks and work insignificant compared to my sister's case.

Pulling out my phone, I closed the door inside the copy room, starting up the flyers I needed to print. The job would take at least twenty minutes—enough time to check in with Agent Phillips.

I dialed his number, impatiently drumming my fingers on the hard plastic lid of the copier.

He answered on the third ring. "Callie. How are you?"

I rolled my eyes at his calm greeting. "Not good. Worried about my sister." I didn't say her name aloud in case the mayor had cameras set up in this room. Wouldn't surprise me if he did. Bree laughed at my paranoia, but Elliot Goodman wasn't a good man. The sneaky bastard was capable of anything. "Any new information?"

"Not much. I can tell you the BAU finished revising the profile for the unsub, and it matches Elliot Goodman."

Of course, it did.

"The unsub works a consistent area that includes Henderson and Las Vegas. A hunting ground where he can easily pick up escorts like Sadie and other working girls. He prefers crowds and clubs where he can disappear without anyone noticing the girls he's trafficking or his other numerous crimes."

"How does this help us?"

"We've been watching the mayor and going through hundreds of hours of camera footage. He frequents the same locations, moving through each one before circling back again."

"Like a shark," I spat.

"Yes, in a way. What's been interesting is who he associates with, the length of the interaction, and how the meetings end."

"I hope you have something promising to share."

"I do," Agent Phillips admitted. "We found Sadie on the tapes the night she disappeared, including all of the men present at the meeting Elliot brought her to and who she left with."

"Who?" I asked, my voice barely above a whisper.

My heart rate picked up, anxiety threatening to choke the breath from my lungs.

"Members of the Dirty Death MC. They didn't bother hiding their leather vests with the emblem."

"They knew about the cameras," I guessed.

"Yes. It didn't faze them."

Not good. They didn't fear the cops or the feds.

"Did she go with them willingly?"

"That isn't an easy answer. I'm inclined to say yes because Sadie wasn't presented with a choice."

Shit.

"So she's being held prisoner by those bikers?"

"I don't know, but I'll find out."

"When?" I asked, sick of the endless wait.

"Tonight." He coughed, lowering his voice. "Listen. I shouldn't be telling you all this, but I don't want you to lose hope. I'm finding Sadie. With any luck, I'll be bringing her home after the raid."

"What if those bikers are waiting for you?"

"It's a possibility I've already considered and have covered."

I didn't need to know the specifics. One thing bothered me, though. "Why didn't this footage show up sooner?"

"Do you know how many clubs and bars there are in Las Vegas?" He chuckled without humor, clearing his throat. "Took longer than I wanted, but we've got what we needed. There's enough here for a search warrant for Elliot's properties, the Dirty Death MC compound, and their known affiliates. It's a big break in the case, Callie."

He sounded tired. I imagined he hadn't slept much since Sadie disappeared. I know I didn't.

I woke up constantly every night, leaving my bed and staring out the sliding glass doors overlooking my back patio and the starry sky, wishing she would show up and end this nightmare.

"I don't think I'll be able to sleep tonight," I replied finally, biting my lower lip as I tried not to focus on all the things that could go wrong.

"You should try. It's going to be a long night."

As if that would change a single thing. "I'll keep the coffee on."

He understood. "Once I have news, good or bad, I'll let you know."

"And if my sister isn't there?"

"We'll get the information we need on Sadie and the other missing women. You have my word."

I didn't envy Agent Phillips or the feds. This case was making headlines on every social media outlet imaginable. People were skittish. Some protested outside the mayor's office in downtown Henderson. City Hall had been bombarded with advocacy groups demanding justice. Wherever I went, I heard people talking about the missing women and the reality of human trafficking in our city. Unfortunately, this was an issue long before the mayor got involved.

"I'll be waiting," I announced, ending the call.

The printer finished the flyers, and I picked the massive pile up, dividing the stack into several bins for the interns to sort.

Hours later, Bree sat with me on a leather couch, reviewing the files she found in the mayor's office. He'd left the door to his safe ajar, and she'd found a ton of incriminating evidence. Skeptical, I had to wonder if the files she found were planted. It seemed too easy.

"I didn't have time to look at what I copied from his computer. I'll go over it later at home when I don't have to look over my shoulder."

Good plan.

"I don't know what I'll find on the USB drive, but the safe I found was full of cash, stacks of documents, and several file folders like he stuffed it all inside in a hurry. Elliot has identification records for some of the employees, receipts for several different Casinos, and photos. Lots of photos."

"What kind?"

"Blackmail photos. Has to be. Look."

She flipped through the stack, showing me shots of a motorcycle club called the Devil's Murder MC.

I frowned. "There are two motorcycle clubs in Henderson?"

Bree shrugged. "Appears so. I know there's the Dirty Death MC too. I've seen them pop up often in the mayor's correspondence. I think he has some kind of longstanding deal with them."

She flipped through the stack of pictures, stopping when she reached the ones with the mayor and his arm around each of the missing girls, including Sadie.

"Oh my god! There he is with my sister!" I snatched it from Bree's hand, staring into Sadie's face. "This is recent. It has to be from the weeks leading up to her disappearance."

"Yeah, I agree." She gestured to the pile in front of us. "This is evidence. We need to give it to your FBI contact."

She was right. This could help my sister's case. I needed to meet with Agent Phillips.

Biting my lip, I stared at Sadie's face next to Elliot, concerned that the mayor had set her up. "She's in trouble, Bree. I know it. What if these bikers are hurting her right now? What if they bury her out in the desert, and I never find her?" Panic clawed at my chest. "I'm never going to see Sadie again!"

"Hey, calm down. We don't know anything yet, but it's enough to share with Agent Phillips and maybe get a search warrant."

Letting my imagination run wild wasn't helping. "You think?" I didn't tell her about Agent Phillips and the plans we discussed. I couldn't.

But now I wondered if he needed to know about this picture and the rest of the snapshots someone had taken. Why did Elliot have all of this in his safe? Did he get sick pleasure knowing these women were all missing and he'd had a hand in their disappearances?

"Yes. We need to log off our computers for the night and get out of this office. It's getting late."

"You're right." I opened my phone, snapping a quick pic of the mayor and Sadie before handing it over to Bree. She arranged everything neatly into the folders, giving me an encouraging smile.

"I'll keep the flash drive, and you should take the physical stuff. Find out if Agent Phillips will meet with you and look at all the information we collected. Let me know what he says."

"Okay. I'll contact him as soon as I'm home."

My fingers gripped the file folders tightly as we gathered our belongings and left the building. We parted ways as we reached our vehicles, waving to one another as we pulled out of the parking lot.

I wondered if Agent Phillips would have what he needed to expose the mayor after this. It seemed like overwhelming evidence of his involvement to me. Enough suspicious documentation to raise a few red flags. That had to help Sadie's case.

Driving home, I felt anxious, wondering if I should wait to reach out to Agent Phillips. He was preparing for the raid on the Dirty Death MC compound and wouldn't have time to mess with bullshit. But this was important. It could mean something big for Sadie and the rest of the missing girls.

Pushing the button for a hands-free call, I dialed Agent Phillips' number.

His gruff voice answered after the first ring. "Callie?"

"I have something you need to see."

FIVE

CALLIE

Present time—

"I EXPECTED YOU TO be more menacing," I admitted, sitting across from Agent Phillips at a booth in one of the greasy spoon diners on the outskirts of Las Vegas. I scooted my ass across the red sticky seat, hoping like hell it was only syrup that gripped my flesh as the material squeaked. "Nice location."

He smirked. "Glad to meet you too, Callie Withers."

"Call me Callie. Oh wait, you already do," I deadpanned, picking up a menu. At least it didn't stick to my fingers.

"You're sassy like your sister." He flashed a grin. "She didn't like me at all when we first met."

I gave the FBI agent a once over, inspecting him from the top of his closely cropped head of dark hair to the muscled, hard body that disappeared below the table.

It wasn't hard to guess why my sister became attracted to this man. He had this cross between a bad boy and a nerd that oddly worked for him.

Lots of dark ink covered his arms, but he wore glasses. Short hair with prescription sunglasses perched on the top but a pen stuck into the pocket of his polo shirt. The tight dark blue material hugged his bulging biceps and tapered down his trim torso. He squinted occasionally and pushed his glasses up his nose when they slipped. Clean, clipped nails on his fingers, but he wore a couple of rings. One looked like an expensive class ring from college. I didn't doubt he had an impressive education.

Agent Phillips kept his body in top physical condition, and he appeared sharp, observant as his gaze flicked around the restaurant, and relaxed but ready to spring into action at a moment's notice.

He fidgeted in his seat, betraying a slight inability to keep still. That was confirmed when he began tapping his fingers, caught himself, and picked up the salt and pepper shakers, moving them back and forth on the table's surface.

"You have ADHD," I observed. Just like Sadie.

He arched a brow.

"Pick up a menu and put the condiments away. You're making me antsy."

A chuckle left his lips as he pushed the shakers away, glancing down at the menu in front of him. "The only thing worth eating here is breakfast. Trust me on that."

I didn't see a reason not to. A man like him probably saw a lot of diners in the early morning hours after putting in a hard night's work on a case. "Okay. I know what I want."

Agent Phillips signaled to the waitress. She walked over, smoothing back her pink hair, and held up a notepad. After she greeted me, she took my order.

"Anything to drink?"

"Coffee and a large orange juice." I thumbed in the agent's direction. "He's buying so one check."

She snickered, leaving us to grab a coffee carafe. Once we had our cups full, she put in our order and checked in with her other customers.

Watching the strait-laced, too-serious man across from me, I wondered what brought him together with my sister. "When did you meet?"

He didn't have to ask. We both knew who I referred to.

"When I interrogated her after Sadie was arrested. She was so pissed at me. Took a swing and hit my jaw." He rubbed it with a tender smile on his face. "She's like no one else I've ever met."

He didn't have that wrong.

"She told me about you," I confessed. "A couple of months before she disappeared."

"Oh?" He seemed surprised but in a good way.

"She said I could trust you, Agent Carson Phillips, because you cared about her, that you were sweet and charming, but you didn't mess around. You followed the rules but would do anything to keep her safe. Is that true?"

"Yes." He pushed his empty mug aside. "You can drop the Agent Phillips moniker. It's stuffy. Just call me Carson."

Nodding, I drank my coffee, almost finishing it. It wasn't nearly as good without Cinnabon creamer, but the hazelnut wasn't terrible. "Why did you agree to meet me tonight?"

"Evidence?" he asked, shrugging.

"I don't think I'm giving you anything new. Am I?"

He shook his head. "No, probably not, but I'll take a look."

The waitress returned with our food, and we ate, pausing the conversation to tuck into our meal. Once I finished, I slid my plate away, noting Carson cleaned his plate and refilled his coffee.

I reached inside my handbag, pulling out the file folders with all the photos and documents I'd gotten from Bree.

Carson reached for the stack, discreetly opening the first folder at an angle to prevent anyone from seeing the contents. He cursed when he saw Sadie and the mayor. "Shit."

"I thought you already discovered this evidence."

"Most of it, yes." He stared longingly down at my sister's face. "Fuck. I miss her."

I couldn't help asking the next question that slipped from my mouth. "Do you think she's still alive?"

He lifted his head to stare into my eyes. Carson didn't flinch or hesitate to answer. "Sadie is intelligent, tough, street smart, and can handle herself in perilous situations. I taught her some self-defense moves, but she had her own way of protecting herself." A brief, wistful smile widened his mouth. "She's the strongest person I've ever met and the most selfless. Sadie would do anything to help the other escorts. Keeping them safe meant everything to her."

"Is that a yes?"

"I believe she could survive almost anything. It's not in her nature to fail," he grunted. "I've become fond of Sadie, but I also respect the brave young woman who wouldn't back down from the dangerous men who tried to control her. She's got an iron will. It's awe-inspiring to learn her story. She's like a phoenix. Sadie will rise from the ashes, and she'll make it home."

What an interesting metaphor. A bit cheesy, but I let him have it.

"You're right. Whatever life throws at my sister, she always perseveres."

He opened his mouth to reply when we heard the rumble of motorcycle engines. A half dozen bikes pulled into the parking lot, parking in a row in front of the diner. Men in leather vests cut the engines, silencing the throaty, growling beasts.

I sucked in a breath, wondering what we should do.

Were these men following us? Did they know I was Sadie's sister and I sat across from an FBI agent?

"Hey, it's okay. These are Devil's Murder MC members, not Dirty Death."

"Does that matter? They're dangerous."

"Anyone can be dangerous. At least bikers don't hide it."

I never thought about it like that.

"Should we leave?"

Carson shook his head. "No. There's no need to feel intimidated."

The group of bearded, heavily inked, wild-looking men pushed through the front door of the establishment, finding a big table in the farthest corner. Not one put his back to the door or aisle. They sat crowded relatively close together, facing the table, backs to the windows. A couple seemed to watch outside for trouble. I bet it followed on their heels with ravenous hunger. Living life as an outlaw had to come with its own warning label.

One guy stood out from the rest. He couldn't have been more than thirty. I'd never seen so many tattoos on a person's face before. The number thirteen appeared twice. Roman numerals on the left. A diamond with the number in the middle on the right. On his forehead, a spiderweb peeked from his hairline. Some symbol I didn't recognize boldly etched in his ear and a cross on the opposite side of his face. Above his left eye, I spotted a word in Greek. Spartan?

The biker kept his brown hair on the shorter side, closely shaven on the sides, but a soft wave wove through the strands. Were his eyes blue or green? I couldn't tell from this distance. Maybe hazel.

A thick beard graced his strong jaw, slightly darker than his hair. A bit scruffy but definitely not unkempt. He didn't let it grow wild.

There were two piercings in his left ear. A silver hoop high in the upper cartilage and a silver cross dangling from the lobe. He rounded out the bad boy look with a thin silver hoop in his right nostril.

Interesting. Actually, sexy as fuck.

His arms and neck were bare, covered in more dark ink. Something about this guy intrigued me. When his head turned, I caught the wolfish grin he flashed.

Shit. He caught me staring. His gaze flittered over me, lingering a few seconds before turning back to his biker friends. Or were those brothers? I really didn't have a clue.

"Callie?"

Double shit. I felt a flush creeping up my neck when I realized I'd been caught staring at a stranger and ignoring the FBI agent I met for breakfast to go over my sister's case. What the hell was I thinking?

"You were saying?" I asked, ignoring the booth with the bikers.

Carson shook his head. "You should stay away from those bikers. They're trouble."

"Because motorcycle clubs have a bad reputation?" I couldn't help the snarky reply.

"No, Callie. They're in a war with the Dirty Death MC. I don't want you to end up in the crossfire."

Swallowing hard, I nodded. "Understood."

Carson picked up the files I'd given him and shoved them into a leather satchel. He snapped the bag closed and rubbed a hand over his jaw. "I think this meeting is over. You need to get back home. It's not safe here."

"Can I ask you a question?"

He hesitated. "Okay. Sure."

"Is the Devil's Murder MC as bad as Dirty Death?"

"Depends on your definition of bad. If you're asking if they bend the law and do as they wish, then yes. If you want to know if they ride around murdering people, that's harder to answer. The burden is proof, and that's something neither club leaves for us to find."

Oh, wow, okay. "You're saying they don't leave witnesses or bodies. No one left to rat them out."

"Maybe." He picked up the check, rising to his feet. "You should leave with me. Don't hang around here alone."

With a sigh, I slid from the booth, slinging my purse across my neck and letting the bag rest against my hip. I followed Carson into the aisle, noting he walked a few steps ahead of me but seemed attuned to the vibe in the diner. The patrons didn't seem too concerned about the bikers in the booth, even if a few people kept glancing their way. I guessed it was curiosity more than fear.

I felt the heated gaze of someone watching me as I walked out, leaving Carson to pay. I'd parked out front, a few spaces from the motorcycles gleaming in the hot Nevada sun. Ten a.m., and it was already scorching hot. I opened my car door, tossing my purse onto the passenger seat, followed by the T-shirt I had worn over my tank top.

Keys in hand, I watched as Carson exited, tucked his glasses into the pocket with the pen, and placed his sunglasses over his eyes.

"See ya around," I called out.

"I'll be in touch." He glared at the diner, and I turned, noticing the group of bikers watching us with interest.

Uh-oh. Maybe this wasn't as discreet as we had hoped.

"Do they know who you are?"

"No clue. Get in your car and drive away, Callie. Now."

Sighing, I planted my ass on the seat of my SUV, rolled down the windows, cranked the latest song by Motionless in White, and sped out of the parking lot.

No one followed me home, not even Carson, but I thought I caught an unmarked car outside the townhomes where I lived and a guy with a crewcut duck down before I entered through the gate, and I unlocked my back door.

For the rest of the night, I stayed indoors.

BREE NEVER RETURNED TO work. After the night we found all that evidence, she disappeared.

Just like Sadie.

To say I was freaking out was an understatement.

I called Agent Phillips for advice, wondering if I should report Bree missing like I did with Sadie. He didn't answer. For several days, I kept calling, finally leaving a couple of frantic messages. He never texted or returned my call.

This couldn't be happening. First, my sister disappeared. Then Bree. Now, Carson ghosted me, or he was missing too. Terrified, I realized I was the only person in contact with all three of them.

Holy. Shit. Was I next?

Pacing my room, I chewed on a nail, jumping at every noise I heard outside. Should I leave? Find someplace to lay low for a bit? What if Sadie showed up and I wasn't here?

No. I couldn't take that chance.

My phone vibrated with an incoming message. I stared at it, relieved to see Bree's name pop up. *Finally.*

I typed a quick response, asking if I could give her a call. I needed to hear Brianna's voice to know she was okay.

She dialed my number first. I almost dropped my phone, swiping across the screen to answer.

"Oh my God, Bree! Are you okay? Why haven't you contacted me? I've been worried sick!"

"It's a long story. My phone got stolen."

"Oh, shit!"

"I know, right?" She sounded tired.

"Tell me you're not in the hospital or anything."

"I'm fine." She didn't sound like it. I caught the way her voice nearly cracked. "Tell me you still have all that evidence we found."

"Yes and no. I gave the files to Agent Phillips, but I also took pics and saved them on my phone. I downloaded everything onto my laptop as a backup."

She seemed relieved. "Good. What did Agent Phillips say?"

I burst into tears, legit bawling into the phone. The stress about my sister and this case was too much. "He's gone, Bree. He's missing. I can't get ahold of him."

"Well, fuck," she cussed, frustrated.

I felt the same way. "Exactly. I hope he's okay."

If the Dirty Death MC found him, he was dead or close to it. I didn't want to think about him hurt or suffering. Maybe he had to ditch his phone in order to track down Sadie's kidnappers.

"Listen, things have gotten a lot more complicated. We need to meet up soon. It's too risky to talk over the phone."

"Okay. Let's do it. Text me the time and place. I'll be there," I promised.

"I'll be in touch. Be careful."

"I will. You too, Bree."

I ended the call, tossing my phone down on my bed. My stomach churned as I wrapped my arms around my middle, trying not to panic. Just because I didn't have all the answers didn't mean everything was hopeless.

Carson would come through. He'd find my sister. I had to believe this would end soon. There wasn't any other choice.

SIX

HAWK

"I DON'T LIKE THIS, pres. Shit's about to blow the fuck up."

Crow scrubbed a hand down his face and over his beard, giving me a nod. "I know."

"Undertaker sent his club to attack Raven. He killed Rook. That motherfucker attacked the Roost. We need to end him. Now."

"That's why I need you to listen. You remember the map we found on the back of those blackmail photos? The ones in the envelope?"

During church a few weeks back, Crow showed us the envelope Bella had given him. We didn't know it at the time, but Undertaker had sent it to mess with us. "Yeah. The map led to your house as a kid. Why?"

"Claw and Jay checked out my old childhood home and found another envelope."

Fuck. "What was in it?"

Crow ran a hand through his hair, clearly agitated. "More photos and a locker key. It's for a locker in a fucking gym. I want you to check it out and bring back whatever is in it."

"Okay, pres. You got it."

"Raven is gonna lose his shit when he sees those photos."

"Shit. Tell me."

Crow shook his head. "It's fucked up. Grudge beating Bree and the mayor getting a blow job as he watched."

Raven's ol' lady. Fuck. "Undertaker and the mayor will regret fucking with our club and women," I snarled.

"There's more," Crow spat, cracking his neck.

Not what I wanted to hear. As security for the club, I provided the primary protection for my brothers and their families. It was my job to ensure this shit didn't happen. But Bree was taken before Raven claimed her, and I couldn't blame myself for her kidnapping or rape. "Give it to me straight, pres."

"It's Undertaker."

"I figured." He found the safehouse where Raven and Bree were staying. We didn't know if we had a rat in the club or not.

"Before Grudge died, he told Raven that Undertaker knew he'd mated Bree."

My body stilled, frozen in shock. "Mated? He said that specific word?" Not wife or ol' lady or girlfriend. Mate. A sacred bond to our crow.

"Yes. There's only one explanation that makes sense. He's got a bond with his animal."

I stared at my pres, thinking he had to be joking, wondering why he specified *animal* instead of *crow*. "Well, shit. You think he's a shifter. Don't you?"

"I do."

"What kind?"

"A wolf."

A wolf? As in werewolf? "Are you fucking serious?"

"Think about it, Hawk. He scented us and followed our club members. Undertaker knows every safe location we have, every home we live in, and everywhere we meet on a regular basis. The Roost. Our family members. All of it. He has the scent of the crows. He can *track* us."

Holy shit!

"We can't let him live," I finally replied. "He'll come after the club and hunt us all down one by one if he needs to. Wolves are relentless predators. If this is true, we need to form a plan."

"I know. We bring this to church. Undertaker wanted a war with us; he's got one. No fucking mercy."

"You tell this shit to Raven yet?"

Crow shook his head. "No. Gonna head in and talk to him now."

"Text me the address of the gym. I'll check it out as soon as I leave here."

"Who's stayin' for security?"

"With Talon gone, I've got Jay and Claw sticking around tonight."

"Good. Follow up when you have the package. Here's the key."

I took it from him, shoving it into the deepest pocket of my cut where I couldn't lose it. "Tell Raven I've got this. We won't let this disrespect and bullshit slide."

"I know, Hawk. Contact me as soon as you pick up the package."

With a sigh, I leaned against the wall, peering through the window as Crow entered, filling in Raven on our conversation. The blinds were open, allowing anyone who walked by to see the identity of whoever was in the room. Not good.

I pulled out my phone and shot him a quick text. He'd close the blinds once he read my message.

"Is he going to make it?"

I turned, so distracted I never noticed anyone else walking in this direction and stared at the pretty blonde at my side, mesmerized by her sweet smile and the dark lashes framing her gray eyes. Something about her seemed familiar, but I couldn't place it.

Swallowing hard, I hoped I didn't sound like an idiot as I repeated myself. "Who-who?"

Nope. Not a fucking idiot, just a goddamn owl.

I felt the crow's presence and his amusement. Cracking my neck, I tried not to let my annoyance show. An SAA should never be that distracted.

"Bree's new man, Raven."

My gaze slid over this girl's ample curves and pear-shaped figure, noting her thick thighs and generous ass. Fuck. I loved a woman with a little extra weight on her frame. She could take a pounding, and I didn't have to worry about slamming into her hip bones. Driving into her soft, warm body would be fucking heaven.

The blonde bombshell pointed to my cut. "You wear the same brand. Devil's Murder MC. You're his biker buddy, right?"

What the fuck? "We aren't buddies," I growled.

She giggled. "Oh, right. Biker brothers."

"Yeah."

"Well, is Raven going to be okay?"

We stood outside the patient room where Raven had been moved once the doctors stabilized him and his injuries weren't life-threatening. There was only so much Falcon, our healer, could do with that much blood loss. Raven's gunshot wound to the stomach almost killed him.

That was how we ended up at the hospital, most of the club taking shifts to watch out for our enemies.

"You a friend of Bree's?"

She flipped her wavy blonde hair over her shoulder. "Her bestie. I'm Callie."

Never heard of her. Oh, wait. Yeah, the chick Bree worked with at the mayor's office—the one with the missing sister.

"Raven needed a blood transfusion, but he's fine. Too fucking stubborn to die."

She snickered. "I'm glad. Bree deserves to be happy."

I gave her my full attention. "Why are—"

The blaring wail of a fire alarm drowned my words. Sprinklers went off overhead and began pouring water, soaking us in only seconds.

"Ahhhhhh," Callie screeched, covering her hair with her hands. Cute, but useless.

This didn't happen by accident. My crow immediately alerted me to danger. I noticed an odd musky odor that reminded me of burnt hotdogs over a campfire. Weird.

I reached for Callie's hand, tugging her out of the hall into one of the empty patient rooms. I had the door shut and her pinned against it, my body caging hers against the wood so fast that she didn't fight me.

"What are you doing?" She pulled on my arm, but I held tight, refusing to release her.

Peeking out the tiny window in the door, I spotted two men wearing Dirty Death MC cuts. Fucking hell. I needed to warn Crow and Raven.

"Hello? What's the matter with you?" Callie asked, getting riled up.

"Shhh. Stay quiet. I'm saving your life," I whispered, tugging her body closer to mine as I moved away from the door.

This room had two ways in and out, and I pulled Callie along, relieved the blinds in this room weren't open. "Follow me."

"You're crazy," she whispered but obeyed, shivering as her wet clothes clung to her body.

I couldn't look down again, or I'd stare at her perky tits and the hard nipples I had already accidentally caught when we rushed inside this room.

"You ever heard of the Dirty Death MC?" I asked, pausing at the door as I heard the water shut off. The floor would be slick. I needed to get us out of here without falling in the process.

"Yes," she whispered, her gray eyes betraying fear.

Fuck. I didn't like her reaction.

"They're here to fuck with my club."

"Shit," she cursed. "In a hospital?"

Undertaker and his club didn't give a fuck. Didn't take a genius to figure that out. Those bastards had been a pain in the ass long before Undertaker ordered the hit on Rook.

"Gonna need you to stick close to me, sweetheart. I'll get you out safely."

She bit her bottom lip, nibbling on the plump surface. Goddamn. Perfect, straight, delicate white teeth absorbed my attention until I blinked.

What the hell?

"You okay?"

Christ. She noticed how I stared, completely losing focus.

"Why wouldn't I be?" I asked, not really expecting an answer.

She responded anyway, shrugging her shoulders. "I don't know you, so I can't answer that question."

Irked, I clasped her hand, dragging her against my body. The warmth of her skin and a soft, feminine scent invaded my senses. Sunflowers. Citrus. *Fucking addicting.*

My palm rose, sliding around her neck as I lowered my head, holding her gently in place. "When we leave this room, I need you to follow my directions. Don't hesitate. Don't fight me. If we're lucky, they won't notice us."

"I don't even know your name."

Why the fuck was that important?

"Hawk," I grumbled, tapping the patch on my cut as I released her. "It's right here."

"You don't have to be an ass," she sassed.

"Well, honey, we don't have time for this shit," I shot back.

"Fine."

I knew enough about women to know the word *fine* never meant things were okay—usually, the opposite. If I wasn't trying to get us out of this hospital without being gunned down by the Dirty Death, I wouldn't be so short with her, but the crow's agitation became my own.

I didn't have the patience for this. My mind flipped to protective mode, and when that happened, I became a cold, ruthless motherfucker on a mission.

We reached the door, and I slid it open a couple of inches, noting the busy hall. Hospital staff rushed around to clean up the mess and check on patients. The chaos allowed the DDMC the chance they needed to search the rooms for Raven, Crow, and any of my other brothers. My phone buzzed in my pocket, and I checked the screen.

Crow: *We're outside. Get the fuck out of there.*

Crow: *Use the key at the gym and pick up the package.*

I shot back a quick response. *On it pres.*

I slipped out of the room, clenching Callie's hand. We moved fast, passing rooms on the floor as I rushed to the stairway at the end of the hall. The elevator was too risky. We didn't have that kind of time.

I caught that strange odor again as we reached the door, and I twisted the handle, guiding Callie inside before shutting it with a soft click.

"Move, sweetheart," I ordered. "They're not far behind us."

Callie gasped, racing down the steps in front of me.

Only three floors stood between us and freedom. My gaze bounced around, landing often on the jiggly, round ass in front of me. What a fuckin' view.

I heard footsteps in the stairwell as we reached the final door. Ushering Callie outside, I walked briskly next to her side, reaching for her hand and curling my fingers around her smooth, soft skin. A tiny jolt sped up my arm, and I almost flinched.

What the hell was that?

Caw...caw.

"Shit," I cursed.

The crow flew above our heads, sweeping in a wide circle as we reached my bike. He sensed danger and sent a warning.

"I know," I mumbled low.

Callie's gaze roamed over my Harley with a frown. She didn't seem like the type to ride but it didn't matter. She'd have to deal with any issues she had once we got the fuck out of here.

"Here. Put this on." I pushed the helmet into her hands and swung my leg over the seat. "Hurry, sweetheart."

She blinked, staring at the black paint on the helmet, then at me. "I don't think this is a good idea."

"Hey, I get you're scared, but we've got to go. Now. I'll take you anywhere you want to go once you're safe. Okay?"

She bit her lip, thinking it over. "This seems reckless. My car isn't far away. Those bikers don't know who I am. If I leave, they won't come after me." She held out the helmet. "I can't leave with you."

Well, fuck. I stood, taking the helmet from her hands. "Babe. You don't get it. I think they already know who you are."

"What?"

"You work with Bree, and they targeted her. I don't think you're safe. You need to—"

"No! I don't believe you—"

I did the only thing I could think of: shut her pretty mouth and get her to listen. My head lowered, and I smashed my lips to hers, drawing her into my chest at the same time. It wasn't supposed to be a kiss that meant anything other than distraction. I shouldn't have deepened the connection, forcing my tongue into her mouth. My cock thickened as the kiss seemed to awaken something primal inside. A need so fierce that I hardly contained it.

I longed to trace the curves of her body with my fingertips and groaned, reluctantly pulling away. Callie's chest heaved, and her eyes closed as she swayed against me. I took advantage of the moment to place the helmet over her head, securing the strap under her chin. "C'mon, beautiful. We need to move. Now."

Her eyes snapped open, cloudy as the sky after a storm. "Hawk—"

She never got a chance to finish her sentence.

A bullet whizzed past her head, lodging into the hospital's stucco façade.

Fuck!

SEVEN

HAWK

CALLIE SCREAMED AS I pulled her to my bike and threw a leg over it, kicking up the stand and starting the engine as a low rumble roared to life beneath me. "Get on!"

She didn't hesitate, slamming her bottom onto the seat and wrapping her arms around my waist.

I sped off, zooming across the parking lot and around a parked ambulance, increasing the speed as I blew by two Dirty Death MC members jumping on their rides.

Fuck. Me.

I heard the engines growling behind us and knew the DDMC was in pursuit. I couldn't let them reach us or get close enough to fire off any shots. Callie was a fucking target behind me. I wasn't allowing her to stay that vulnerable or end up hurt because of me or the club.

61

We whipped out of the parking lot at top speed, making a wide arc down the street and around the block, straight through a red light. Cars honked as I lowered my head, concentrating on the intersection looming ahead. If only it was the middle of the night, I wouldn't have to worry about any of these cages ramming into us.

There were too many fucking vehicles on the road.

I steered the bike to the left, rolling up over the curb as Callie squealed, gripping my cut as we caught air for about two seconds, slamming back down on the asphalt with a vicious jerk. The rear tire fishtailed, and my bike swerved, but I didn't slow down.

We rode over the sidewalk, barreling through pedestrians like they were fucking pins in a bowling alley. No, I didn't hit anyone, but they sure dived out of the way. Smirking, I rolled the throttle toward me and shifted gears, grunting as the engine revved. I thought I heard a gunshot as something bit into my side, but I ignored the sting, focusing on weaving in and out of the traffic.

Behind us, I heard a crash and knew the Dirty Death wasn't far behind. "Hold on!" I shouted, spotting the oversized semi pulling out of a restaurant and onto the road. If I timed this right . . .

The truck driver honked as we cut him off, finishing his turn as he yelled out his window at us. Callie smacked my arm as I laughed, relieved to find the other motorcycles couldn't follow us yet. We needed to lose them, but the desert didn't hide much. All I needed to do was confuse our scent and wait it out, hoping they'd give up with the evening crowd. If Crow was right, those Dirty Death members were trackers.

The Downtown commercial corridor, known as the Water Street District, was a place to shop, dine, and visit the casinos. If we could reach the parking garage off Market Street, I could find a place for us to hide my bike. There was a bar friendly to the club. They'd provide cover for a few hours until nightfall.

I rolled into the garage for one of the casinos as Callie shouted.

"You're bleeding!"

Fuck. I guess one of those fuckers managed to graze me.

"I'll live," I announced, maintaining speed as we rode up a ramp, traveling upward until we reached the highest level. Thanks to the weekend, there weren't any empty spaces. I found a big suburban parked in a row with other SUVs—the perfect vehicles to hide my bike.

"Hop off, honey. Give me a minute to stash our ride."

She slipped off on shaky legs, hugging her torso as I carefully maneuvered my bike against the back wall, hidden where the light wasn't as bright. The inner portion of the garage was far dimmer and would provide the discretion I needed.

I hissed as I stood, shaking off the numb feeling in my head. Dizzy, I stood still a few seconds before reaching inside to find the tarp I kept in my panniers. Covering my bike only took a minute, but the effort weakened me. I'd lost more blood than I realized.

With a groan, I stumbled toward Callie.

"Hawk!" She rushed toward me, pressing her hand against my side as I winced.

"I think there's a bullet by my ribs," I joked.

"Oh my god! How can you joke about that?"

My lips widened into a grin. "You worried about me, baby?"

She rolled her eyes. "You need medical attention, and we just left a hospital."

"We can't go back either."

"I'm aware," she snarked. "What do we do? You're bleeding everywhere!"

"Nah. I just need you to make a bandage."

She stared at me like I spoke a different language. "How am I supposed to do that?"

"Well," I began, staring at her tits and unable to hide my appreciation, "if you rip off the bottom half of that tank top, I bet it would work."

She glanced at the white tank she wore, blinking at me as she considered it.

"Or I can keep bleeding. Up to you, beautiful."

"Shit," she cursed with her silky soft lips that I suddenly wanted to kiss again. She attempted to rip the material, and nothing happened. "Do you have a knife?"

"Sure do," I realized, swaying slightly on my feet. Reaching into my cut, I grasped the knife and slapped it into her palm. "Don't cut yourself, babe."

She narrowed her eyes. "You're calling me a lot of pet names."

"I like the way they sound on my tongue. In the same way I'd like to see if you taste as delicious as you look."

Oops. I said that part out loud instead of in my head.

A giggle escaped as she shook her head, using the blade to cut around her middle until she had a jagged but serviceable bandage. Creamy skin snared my attention as I reached out and slid a finger over her navel and up her ribcage.

Callie sucked in a breath. "Hawk. I need to wrap you up."

Right. My hand dropped, and I shrugged off my cut, followed by my shirt. "You gotta hold my cut. It never touches the ground."

She bit her lip and nodded, sticking her arms through the sleeves as she grabbed it. I had to fucking pause because seeing this sexy, fine woman wearing my leather turned me the fuck on.

"Fuck, Callie. You make me want an ol' lady."

"I don't know what that means. Lift your arms so I can get a look at your wound."

I held onto my shirt and obeyed, biting into the inside of my cheek at the fresh wave of pain slicing into my side.

Callie lowered her head, examining the gunshot wound. "It's deep. I don't know how you're standing right now. There's blood all down your side. People are going to notice."

"They won't. You'd be surprised how distracted people are and how much detail they miss. Too absorbed in their lives to pay attention. Plus, my jeans are dark denim."

She gave me a look like she doubted my words. "Maybe. You would snag my attention, though."

I couldn't help grinning at that. Did she realize what she just admitted? This sexy woman found me attractive.

"What do you want me to do?"

"Take my shirt and press it against the hole in my side. Then use the bandage. Not too hard to figure out, honey. It's not brain surgery."

She glared at me and folded the shirt. I held it to my side, then stretched the material around my middle, just enough left over to tie it.

"Make sure it's tight," I added, enjoying the flush in her cheeks as I riled her up a bit.

"That's going to hurt."

"And slow down the bleeding." My hands fisted as she finished, breathing through the pain because I couldn't pass out until we were safe. Goddamn. The entire left side of my body burned. Sweat beaded on my brow.

Don't be a pussy, Hawk.

"This isn't going to work for long," she worried.

"I know. We just need to get to the Powder Keg."

"What's that?"

"A bar owned by a friend. He'll take care of us." I lifted my knuckles to brush along her cheek. "You're doing great, Callie. Fucking amazing, baby. Just keep it up a little longer, okay?"

Her lower lip quivered, but she straightened her spine. "Okay."

"Take off my cut and turn it inside out, then help me put it on. It'll help hide my wound."

Once I had it on, she reached for the zipper. "You want this zipped?"

"Yeah, better do it." The two-way zipper proved quite convenient right now.

Once done, she smiled. "You look handsome, Hawk. Like we're here on a date."

Smirking, I had to laugh at that. "Never been on a date."

"Why not?"

"I was only interested in fucking, nothing more. Dating seemed a waste of time. Either a chick wants my dick, or she doesn't."

My blunt response didn't shock her as much as I expected. Yeah, I said that shit on purpose to see how she'd take it.

"You're missing out. Dates are fun." She shrugged. "Which way?"

I took a step in her direction, slipping an arm around her waist. "Does that mean you're down to fuck?" Yep, teasing her was gonna be way too much fun.

She smacked my chest, and I winced.

"Omg, sorry!"

"Is that a no?" I lifted my hands when she swatted at me, chuckling at her heated cheeks. My gaze locked on hers, noticing the stormy gray had darkened. Was that lust? "Tell me you're not thinking about my cock right now."

"You're idiotic. Shot, bleeding, and still thinking with the wrong head."

"You bring out the beast in me."

Caw...caw.

And the crow agreed.

About time he showed up. Where the fuck had he flown off to since those Dirty Death chased us? Goddamn crazy bird.

Callie blew out a breath. "Where's the Powder Keg?"

"I'll tell you for a kiss."

"You can't be serious right now."

I slapped my hand over my chest. "As serious as a heart attack."

This girl wasn't like anyone I ever met. Feisty. Intelligent. Sharp-witted. So. Fucking. Beautiful. Not to mention she could handle herself in a crisis.

Ol' lady material.

And I swore I'd never have one. I enjoyed a different woman in my bed every night. Hell, I had a rotation of sweet butts in my room all week at the Roost. Sometimes more than one partner at a time. Adventurous sex turned me on.

Until I stared at this sweet, sexy blonde and her pouty, perfect lips. Gray eyes full of mystery and a hint of mischief. Hourglass curves I itched to grab onto and an ass I couldn't wait to nibble on. She would take my dick like a good girl and love every minute.

Shiiiiit. I needed her, and the idea of seducing her became an instant obsession.

Callie kept me on my toes, and I liked that she wasn't predictable. Too much of my life and the women in it had been a revolving door of the same parties, sex, drugs, and alcohol. No stability other than the club. The Devil's Murder was family, make no mistake about that, but I wanted more than busting a nut and sleeping alone each night.

Holy fuck.

When the hell did that change?

"I don't think this is the time—" Callie began.

I cut her off, tilted her chin, and pressed my lips to hers. A part of me wanted to ravage her mouth and dominate the entire kiss from start to finish, but I didn't. I caressed her mouth like I wanted to do with her cunt, licking, savoring, enjoying the warmth and raw need that suddenly burst into flame. I didn't realize I'd moved us and had her pressed up against the wall until her hands pushed at my chest, severing our connection.

Her chest rose and fell as she struggled to regain her composure. "We can't do this. Not now."

"Later?" I asked with a wink, lightening the moment.

She didn't respond. "Where's the Powder Keg?"

"Make a left out of the garage, walk two blocks, turn left again. You can't miss the big barrel on the neon sign."

She scrunched up her nose. "Okay, about ten minutes. Maybe twelve with your injury."

"You're fucking brilliant, baby."

"I'm not a baby." She made a face like she had just sucked on a lemon. "That's the worst endearment."

"Oh, is it?" Damn. Wasn't she fucking cute? "What do you prefer I call you in bed, baby?"

She closed the distance between us. "Your goddess. Beautiful. Sweetling. Your treasure. Your queen. The list is endless."

The husky way her voice dripped each of those words went straight to my dick, and all the blood rushed south. Instant stiffy. This girl gave me wood I hadn't had since my teen years.

Fuck. Me.

"You ready to leave now, Hawk?"

Nodding, I reached for her hand, tugging her as close as possible. "I don't know what we'll find, but we should be ready to run if necessary."

She pursed her lips. "You won't be running anywhere. You're only standing because of a potent mixture of adrenaline, lust, and the will to survive."

"You talk so pretty, sweetling."

"That's not all I can do."

With a grin, I led us out of the garage, taking much longer than anticipated. Callie wasn't wrong. Now that I was no longer distracted, each step felt heavier than the last. I could feel the blood soaking into my shirt and beginning to drip downward.

If we didn't reach the Powder Keg soon, I would collapse.

My vision tunneled as I swallowed, noticing my dry mouth. Spots darted in and out of my peripheral. Sweat trickled down my temples as I stumbled, leaning against Callie as we walked.

"I've got you. Keep going. We're almost there."

Liar. We'd only gone about half the distance.

At the next corner, I panted, slamming into the wall of a building and nearly crashing to the ground. "Go, Callie. You're close. Tell them where to find me."

"No way! I'm not leaving you."

"You can't stay out here. It's too dangerous. Go. I'll be right behind you," I slurred.

A couple walked our way, and Callie pressed her body against mine, giggling. "Babe. You had too much to drink. Let's get back to the hotel."

They were too caught up in each other to notice us, but Callie's quick thinking avoided a spectacle. When she leaned back, I frowned. My blood had smeared on her stomach and tank top.

"Gorgeous, you've got a little of my essence on you."

"What a time to make a joke. C'mon, Hawk. We're not stopping until we reach the Powder Keg." She pulled on my arm, wrapping it around her shoulders. "Move. Now."

Could you fall in love at first sight? Wasn't that the most cliché, ridiculous, cheesy shit anyone ever came up with? How the fuck could you find your soul mate in a single afternoon?

My mind awakened as the thought lit up my brain.

Not just a soul mate. No ordinary bond. No.

A mate. The forever mate of a crow.

Stunned, I concentrated on moving one foot after another, trying hard not to crush Callie with my full weight. She couldn't have been more than five foot six, and I towered over her at six foot four. My goddess. My curvy dream girl.

I didn't even know I wanted her until I met Callie.

My brain fired in all directions, consumed with the knowledge unlocked in my head. What the fuck did this mean?

Caw...caw.

The crow's ebony wings spread outward above us, sensing the connection I just formed. He chittered in the sky, squawking out a raspy, celebratory kraa.

My muddled thoughts struggled to comprehend the moment fully. I'd lost too much blood. As we reached the bar, I slipped to the ground as my legs gave out, careful not to pull Callie down with me.

She cried out my name, but I couldn't muster the energy to move. "You have to get up, Hawk. Please."

That wasn't possible.

"Get help, gorgeous."

My eyelids drooped as I slumped against the wall. Somehow, we made it to the entrance of the Powder Keg.

"Ask for Marcus."

If she replied, I never heard it.

EIGHT

GALLIE

"Is HE GOING TO be okay?" I asked, pacing the room where Marcus and his bouncers had brought Hawk.

The Powder Keg seemed like a typical bar until I got ushered through a series of rooms, some of them with private parties, stripper poles, and people engaging in sexual acts. Like right out in the open. On furniture. Against the wall.

A woman pleasuring three men on a pool table.

What the hell? Was this a porn studio or something? Did hidden cameras record all of this for entertainment?

"I've contacted Falcon. He'll know what to do."

"Falcon?" I asked, perplexed.

"A healer."

Like a doctor? Hawk needed that bullet removed and the wound sewn by a professional.

I hoped Marcus knew what the big wounded biker wanted because I didn't have a clue.

Hawk groaned but didn't open his eyes as Marcus turned him onto his stomach. He pulled a knife from his pocket and leaned toward the leather vest Hawk wore.

"Don't you dare cut into that," I ordered, stomping over to Marcus. "That's sacred to him."

Marcus smirked. "Alright. Help me remove it."

Carefully, we balanced Hawk and removed the vest, draping it over a nearby chair. Marcus tossed the blood-soaked shirt into the trash, bellowing for a bottle of whiskey. He checked on the wound, nodding as someone brought him a first aid kit along with a bottle of dark amber fluid. I watched as he doused Hawk's side with the liquor and then patted the skin dry. He placed a new bandage over the wound and added the one I'd made from my shirt to the trashcan with the other supplies he had discarded.

I stood a few feet to the side, anxious, staring at the exposed back of sculpted muscle. Tanned skin caught my attention briefly, but it was the dark ink I couldn't help but admire. Black feathers formed giant wings spreading out from Hawk's shoulder blades and reaching outward to the edges of his torso. The exquisite detail made them appear real, as if you could blink, and they would sprout free from his body and help him take flight.

Breathtakingly beautiful. I never saw a tattoo as ideally suited to someone as this one. I thought of the crow that seemed to shadow Hawk wherever he went this afternoon, even following us to the Powder Keg. The man I'd met harbored dark secrets and an affiliation with a dangerous motorcycle club. Yet his playful, teasing nature and passionate responses contradicted the image I'd conjured in my head about bikers.

I couldn't help my attraction to this man. He placed my safety above his own and insisted on protecting me from the Dirty Death and Undertaker.

I knew nothing about that club, only the rumors and minimal evidence I uncovered with Bree. But knowing they worked with the mayor was enough.

My thoughts drifted to the words Hawk said as we left the hospital. *I think they already know who you are.*

Of course! It made sense. Even if the mayor hadn't figured it out, Undertaker probably knew about me. Maybe he used my safety as a threat against Sadie. She would do anything to prevent the Dirty Death MC from harming me if she believed I was in danger. Even sacrificing herself.

Shit. Now I had a whole new set of concerns and worries.

On a whim, I pulled out my cell and dialed Carson's number. No change. Straight to voicemail.

Sighing, I watched as Marcus crossed the room, talking to a few of his men. He ticked his head in my direction.

"Falcon's here. He'll fix Hawk good as new."

"Uh, thanks."

The biker who walked into the room wearing a Devil's Murder MC vest seemed like he should be in a hospital wearing a white coat instead. He wore jeans and a shirt with thick stripes of varying shades of blue but none of the chains or chunky rings or piercings that adorned Hawk's body. Another biker who didn't fit a stereotype. I liked that.

Falcon walked to the bed, his gaze roaming over me from head to toe before he nodded. "You're not injured. That's good. Hawk wouldn't like it if anyone harmed you."

How the hell did he know that?

"I'm Falcon, as you probably guessed. I'm good at puzzles and first aid. If you're here, you mean something to Hawk. That's none of my business, but I'd like to check on him."

I moved out of his way, settling on the opposite side of the bed to observe without being in Falcon's way. "He got shot trying to protect me. We would have gotten out of there if I hadn't been so stubborn."

"Don't lay the burden on yourself, honey. Those men intended to shoot Hawk, and they did. Not a single part of that had anything to do with you."

I couldn't agree. Guilt for taking too long to join him allowed those Dirty Death members to get close.

"I need to dig out that bullet." He stood, gathering supplies from a bag he had brought with him. "Scrub in. I'll need your help."

I assumed he meant washing my hands and scrubbing underneath my nails, so I left Hawk's side, slipping off the mattress. The adjoining bathroom to this room had an enormous double sink. Once I finished thoroughly cleaning my hands, I returned, asking how I could help.

"He's going to be madder than a hornet's nest. It'll hurt and probably wake him up when I start. Be prepared."

For what? I couldn't hold Hawk down if he decided to react violently or push us away.

Falcon must have sensed my unspoken question. "If he wakes up, start talking to him. Your voice will soothe and distract him enough that I can finish."

"Okay." I didn't see how that was possible, but it couldn't hurt to try.

"Do you think you can keep him propped on his side while I work?"

"Sure." That sounded far more confident than I felt. Settling next to Hawk, I gripped his shoulder as he faced me. His body leaned in my direction, one arm resting between us on the mattress.

Once Falcon's knife dug below Hawk's skin, it didn't take long for his eyes to snap open. "Fucking hell!"

"Stay still, you crazy fucker. I've got my knife in your side."

"What the hell for!?"

"The bullet in your flank, far too close to your intestines, remember?"

Hawk grunted, his head flopping back onto the pillow. He stared at the ceiling for about two seconds before his gaze swept the room, landing on me. "Callie. You're not hurt, right? You okay?"

"I'm fine." Staring into his hazel eyes that seemed almost green today, I hesitated to move since I didn't want to disturb Falcon and cause Hawk further pain.

"You look worried, beautiful. I'll be fine." He cursed, gritting his teeth. "Are you fucking done yet, Falcon?"

"Almost."

I smirked at Hawk's bravado. "You can admit it hurts."

"And appear weak to the sexy goddess at my side? No way."

He remembered every endearment I mentioned and made a point to call me every single one. What a flirt.

I loved it. It wasn't hard to become attracted to him when he made me smile so darn much. "Well, at least your humor is returning."

He winked, then grimaced. "Fucking hell."

"There! Got it," Falcon declared. He dropped the bloody bullet on the nightstand. "Let me get you sewed up."

"Finally," Hawk mumbled.

"Should I keep my hands on him?" I asked Falcon.

"Yes, please," Hawk answered with a broad smile.

Falcon smirked. "Yeah. He needs help with that giant ego of his."

"Don't be jealous," Hawk quipped, reaching out to cradle the side of my face. A slight frown marred his brow. "You look tired. Need a nap? We've got this big bed."

Falcon snorted. Hawk ignored him.

"Maybe later. He's about to stick a needle and thread into your skin and stitch you up. I think I should stay awake for that."

I had to stifle a yawn, realizing the day had taken a toll. Exhaustion was creeping in.

"Eh, I've had worse." His fingertips gently caressed my jaw. "It's normal after the adrenaline dump to feel tired."

"Your world is a bit crazy."

"Not with you in it."

I blinked, noting the serious expression on his face. "You sound like you mean that."

"I do."

"We just met," I pointed out, glancing at Falcon as he continued stitching Hawk's wound closed. "Isn't this a bit fast?"

"No one said you gotta marry me, beautiful."

I thought over his words. "What are you asking of me?"

"Let me protect you until the threat is eliminated."

"And afterward?"

"We'll figure that out when it's time."

"That's a vague answer."

He grimaced as Falcon finished up. "I guess you'll just have to let things happen naturally, sweetling."

"I'll think about it."

"What's there to think about?"

"A lot. You're too charming, and you like to flirt. I'm watching you, Mr. Biker."

Falcon chuckled. "I like her. She doesn't put up with your shit."

Hawk flipped him off.

I couldn't help giggling.

Falcon slapped a square bandage over Hawk's side. "All done, precious. You should heal without a scar."

Hawk winced. "You're an ass, Falcon."

"You fucking love me."

"You bet I do, brother."

"Awww. Should I leave you alone for the bromance?"

"Don't you dare." Hawk's hand rested on my hip, tugging me a little closer. His eyes closed briefly and snapped open. "Stay."

"I will," I promised, fighting off my own fatigue.

"You should both rest. I'll be around if either of you needs me. Doc's orders."

"Thanks, Falcon."

My eyes drifted shut, and I relaxed, snuggling as close as I dared into Hawk's warmth without causing him any discomfort. As I slipped into a peaceful slumber, I thought I heard Hawk whisper my name, followed by the word *mine*. No man had ever tried to claim me.

Maybe I'd give Hawk a chance.

HAWK

WHEN I OPENED MY eyes, I could see night had fallen. The room had darkened, and only shadows populated the space beyond the bed.

I inhaled a deep breath, relieved not to feel the same level of pain as I had before Falcon arrived. He did good. My body would take some time to finish the healing process, but it wouldn't be long. Falcon's healing energy soaked into my skin as he removed the bullet and stitched up the wound, ensuring I could leave this bar on my own within a few hours.

Perfect. I had shit to do once Callie was safe.

I'd deal with the Dirty Death and the fucker that shot me, but for now, I focused on the delicate scent of citrus, sunshine, and female.

A soft sigh escaped as Callie rolled onto her back. My hand slipped from her upper abdomen to her lower belly. I let my palm rest there, wondering what it would be like to put a baby inside her and watch my child grow in her womb.

Wait. What the fuck?

When the hell did that thought form in my head? Nu-uh. I didn't want kids. Shit. I didn't want an ol' lady. I had a terrible fucking father, and there was no way I would be good at it.

What the hell was happening to me? Where did all these mushy feelings come from?

I yanked my hand away, forming a fist. This shit was too much.

Mate. The word popped into my head.

Nope. I wasn't indulging in this. I got carried away yesterday. Too much adrenaline and shit. It meant nothing. I wasn't looking for anything but a good time. Get my dick wet, and get the fuck out. I didn't need—

Callie's pretty gray eyes slowly opened, and a tiny smile formed on her lips. "Hi."

My hand relaxed. "Hey."

"How are you feeling, Hawk?"

Fuck. Me.

Her raspy, sleep-laden voice did wicked things to my body. My cock agreed, swelling with the idea that keeping Callie between the sheets until I knocked her up was a fantastic idea.

I was so fucked. So. Fucked.

"All good," I croaked.

"You sure? You sound pained."

Oh, I was, but not like she thought.

My dick was so fucking hard that I could use it like a goddamn hammer right now. I ached to plunge into her pussy and feel her clench around me.

Stop thinking about sex, you stupid motherfucker.

"I'm fine," I lied, watching as her little pink tongue swept across her bottom lip. Christ. Why was that so fucking sexy?

The thought that Callie didn't have a lot of sexual experience popped into my head. I hoped she wasn't a virgin. That shit was too much to deal with. But then the idea of it turned me on even more. Fuck. I'd like to be the only man she let between those thick, toned thighs.

Holy shit. I needed to get a fucking grip on myself.

"I wonder where Falcon went." I had to change the subject. Think about anything other than Callie and how badly I wanted her. Puppies. Rain. A cloudy sky. Gray eyes. Callie!

Shit!

My Harley. Riding into the wind. The rumble of my bike's engine. The smell of gasoline. Warm breath on the back of my neck. A sexy voice saying my name. Callie!

For fuck's sake.

Her gaze locked on mine. "I think he's at the bar." Her soft fingers reached out and rested on my hand. "You seem agitated."

She wasn't wrong.

"Just thinking about Undertaker and his club."

Yeah, that did it—no more thoughts of sex with Callie.

"I don't blame you. They shot you!" She looked upset.

Damn. I didn't like her feeling that way. "Hey, it's gonna be alright. You'll see."

"That's not what worries me, Hawk."

"What's on your mind?" I asked, tugging her close enough to feel her tits pressing against my chest. *Dirty fucker.*

"You said they probably know who I am since I worked at the mayor's office. Does that mean they'll come after me now?"

Sonofabitch.

"I hope not, but if they do, they'll have to go through my whole fucking club to get to you. And that's only if I'm not still breathin', Callie."

She shook her head. "I think they have my sister."

Fuck. I forgot all about her missing sister. "Why do you believe that?"

"Because Sadie is an escort for the DOLL Agency. She got too close to the mayor. He's been using her services, and she disappeared, just like the others. Bree found evidence that he's been working closely with the Dirty Death MC and an unknown entity trafficking girls out of Nevada. That's not all, though. My sister mentioned Undertaker's name. Sadie said she met him, and he liked her. What if she learned something she wasn't supposed to know?"

Sadie. It couldn't be the same girl. No fucking way.

"You have a sister named Sadie? What's your last name?" I sat up, pulling Callie beside me. "It's important."

"Withers. Sadie Withers."

Mind*fucking*blown.

I turned, jumping up from the mattress to pick up my cut, pointing to my road name. HAWK. "You see this?"

"Of course, I have, Hawk. What are you trying to say? I don't, oh wow. No way." She scrambled from the bed, connecting the dots. "You're the biker that saved Sadie? The one who beat Jed's ass?"

Nodding, I swallowed loudly, wondering how we both missed this before now. Of course, I didn't remember ever hearing her sister's name, and she didn't mention it until now. Still, what a small fucking world. "Yeah. I sure the fuck did. The abusive fucker got what he deserved."

Callie rushed in my direction, throwing her arms around me.

"You went to jail and helped a woman you didn't know. You vindicated her and set my sister on a better path. Jed probably would have hunted her down and killed her if you didn't intervene that day." She lifted her head, staring into my face as tears slipped down her cheeks. "I don't know how to thank you enough for what you did. You saved the person I love most in this world. You're my hero, Hawk."

I didn't know how to respond. "I only did what needed to be done. It wasn't a hard decision. I'm no hero, beautiful, but it sure strokes my ego that you think so," I joked.

Compliments made me uncomfortable. Maybe that originated from my old man and how he always tried to make me feel beat down, worthless, and stupid. Took a lot of years to believe all that shit wasn't true. Sometimes I still struggled with the verbal abuse more than the physical.

My head lowered, and my lips brushed Callie's in a tender kiss. "I don't like to see those pretty eyes shed tears. It's just not right."

She tried to smile and failed. "I need your help, Hawk. I have to find Sadie before it's too late. You're the only one who understands what she's up against. I can't lose her."

No. I couldn't let that happen. My choice five years ago ensured my involvement, and it was too late to turn my back now. Not that I would.

The sisters needed a miracle. They got one. A biker, sinner, and outlaw. A man society deemed a villain. But fuck if I wasn't the perfect asshole to get the job done.

"You won't. I'll raise hell to bring her back to you."

NINE

UNDERTAKER

"FUCK. JUST LIKE THAT. Don't stop."

My fingers grazed the cut slut's skull, moving her head back and forth on my cock as I fucked her mouth. She slobbered all over my dick, saliva dripping from her chin in long sticky strands. Her eyes bulged as I shoved in deeper, slamming into the back of her throat.

The sounds she made. Like she was about to choke and couldn't breathe. Fucking beautiful.

I reached down, pinching her nose as she began to panic, sputtering around my girth. Her slim body jolted with every snap of my hips. I kept up the brutal pace growing excited as her body grew limp. She almost lost muscle control.

"I'm going to come. You swallow every fucking drop," I ordered, tugging her head back until the glazed look in her eyes began to disappear. "I want to see my cum sliding down your throat."

Her neck bulged as I pumped a few more times.

With a growl, I unloaded, coming so fucking hard that I couldn't stop, filling up her mouth and throat as she struggled to obey. Milky fluid spilled out of the corners of her lips as she repeatedly swallowed, shoving the cum back up from her chin and trying to stuff it into her mouth.

Fucking hilarious.

I slapped her lips with my dick, spurting a few more times before I finally finished. Sure, the release felt good, but not exceptional. Never would. Not unless I mated.

A fucking curse if you asked me.

I shoved the bitch away from me, disgusted. She was nothing more than a hole to fill. I hated the sight of her.

"Leave," I spat. "Send in your cousin."

The girl shook her head. "Please. You can fuck me anywhere you want. Just not her."

Did I fucking stutter? Hell no.

"Are you refusing me?" I roared, pissed I had to deal with this shit when I had enough on my mind. Fucking Devil's Murder MC was making my life difficult. I hated those cocky motherfuckers.

"No-no," she stammered.

I didn't think so. "Tell her to come naked. I need to fuck some pussy."

My libido always grew unbearable when I got pissed or agitated. I had to fuck the restless beast into submission. Not much else subdued him except for bloodshed. He fucking loved the hunt. Ripping flesh apart and gobbling up the organs kept him satisfied and healthy, but I couldn't go around killing people every fucking day. He loved the kill more than feeding, and that had become an obsession.

Maybe I shouldn't have embraced the vargulf.

Too late to fucking regret it now.

"Go!" I shouted when the girl didn't listen.

She ran from the room, choking on a sob as she went.

Fuck. The monster inside loved the scent of fear. I inhaled, taking in the spicy, slightly acrid odor. So fucking intoxicating. A fucking aphrodisiac. Excitement stimulated my cock, and I stiffened, swelling with lust.

By the time the girl's cousin entered the room, I danced on the edge of my control. This wouldn't be gentle. Of course, it never was. The beast fucked. He needed wild and uncontrolled sex, submissive women he could dominate.

I let my thoughts slip to my prisoner. She didn't invade them often because I coveted her and didn't want to share. I had grown possessive over my pretty doll. Her life became mine as a debt. And oh, how that excited me.

The beast enjoyed knowing she belonged to us.

"Fetch my bride," I ordered as I stuck my head outside the door, barking my orders to my beta who also happened to be my new VP. I demanded loyalty and obedience both as the leader of my pack and the president of this club.

He dipped his chin. "Yes, Alpha."

I growled, pacing as I waited for the women. The first arrived. A petite blonde with a tight ass I already enjoyed several times this week. "On all fours," I snarled, watching as she climbed the bed, assumed the position, and her body quivered. Fear. Desire. They formed a strange scent entangled together.

Delicious.

"Play with your pussy while you wait for me."

I continued to pace, ignoring my cock as it bobbed with every step, swollen, hungry, waiting to unleash his fury.

Just as I thought my patience would snap, she entered—my darling captive.

"Hello, Sadie," I practically purred, struck by her beauty.

"Undertaker."

My hand rose, fisting my erection. Slowly, I began to stroke.

She didn't react.

The perks of being an escort. Nothing sexual usually fazed her. I'd have to change that once I claimed her.

"I want you to watch while I fuck."

"As you wish."

She never denied or sassed me. Her years with the DOLL Agency had taught her exactly how to please a man without ever allowing him to dominate her spirit. Such a remarkable, rare trait few women possessed yet alone wielded. This temptress could handle it all with finesse.

There was something different about Sadie. A bond I sensed could form between us. A link I had never been able to feel with any other creature or human. She would be ripe, her womb open, ready to receive me, and her body would welcome me into her depths. I could breed her, fuck her, and mate her. The shock and thrill of it still pulsed through my veins since the moment I figured it out.

Mine. All fucking mine.

This angel belonged to the devil.

"I'd like you to masturbate while I fuck her."

"Yes, Undertaker."

Sadie sat on a nearby chair, spreading her long luscious legs open as she lifted the hem of her dress, pushing it close to her waist. I spotted the perfect outline of her pussy through her silk panties, lost to the beast and his carnal needs as I salivated.

Her fingers began to swirl her clit, and I groaned.

My body trembled while I positioned myself behind the girl on the bed, unaware of her name or unwilling to learn it. Only Sadie mattered.

Shaky fingers played with her clit, but I smacked them away, taking my cock in hand and sliding from base to tip. The excitement and expectation rolled through me.

Without warning, I slammed inside the girl, unleashing the monster's sexual aggression unrestricted. I fucked her so hard I heard her teeth click together, forcing her head to the mattress.

My hips pistoned, driving into her even when I spotted the drops of blood on the sheets. They spurred on the beast, coaxing him into a partial transformation. My claws lengthened. My mouth ached as I felt my teeth sharpen. My vision enhanced, heightened awareness brightening the room.

I looked down, watching my dick plunging in and out of the girl, transfixed by the blood coating my length, staining my dick with every brutal thrust. Too bad it wasn't because she couldn't take me. No. I had her in my bed all week because her monthly cycle began, and I loved to fuck a bloody cunt.

My head lifted, and I locked eyes with Sadie, watching her hips as they moved in tandem with mine, the rhythm we found together exciting and sensual. It wasn't hard to imagine her body beneath me, taking every inch as I pumped harder. She never tried to hide her reactions or deny her body's desires. Another reason I needed her to be mine.

When her nipples grew hard, straining against the material of her dress, I knew she was close. Her hormones saturated the room with her sweet, sharp scent, like cloves and anise. Someday I would have my tongue inside her when she came.

Her soft cries filled my ears, blocking out any other noise. I gripped the girl's hips on the bed, pulling her back against my thighs as I pounded into her pussy. Vaguely, I heard her screaming as blood gushed around my cock. Her cum disgusted me. I only wanted the woman across the room, staring at me with a hunger that matched mine.

Well, fuck. Maybe her appetites were a wickedly perfect match for a beast.

That thought brought me to completion, jerking as I filled the hole I needed but didn't truly desire. My nails and teeth returned to normal, no longer embracing the partial shift. The room darkened. When I pulled out, I chuckled at the stretched, loose flesh left behind.

Sniffing, I sensed her period had ended. She no longer served a purpose.

"Go," I snapped. "Get out of my bed."

The girl rushed to obey, dripping fluids as she stumbled from the room.

I turned to Sadie, flopping down on the bed. My cock remained engorged, ready to go again if I wanted.

Satisfied for now, I patted the mattress. "Sleep next to me."

She arched a brow.

"Do it. I'll keep our bargain."

No touching her until she asked me.

"If you like," she answered, smoothing her dress over her hips. "I won't deny you."

Fuck. That phrase got to me every time she said it.

"You please me," I stated, stifling a yawn.

"Good."

Her sweet smile was the last thing I saw before closing my eyes, allowing my body to seek the rest it needed.

Did I trust her? No. But that only inflamed my obsession.

HAWK

"WE NEED TO MAKE a small detour," I announced as I uncovered my bike in the parking garage.

"Where?"

She didn't ask why, although I could see the question burning in her eyes.

"I need to pick up a package at a local gym. It'll be quick. Something for my pres, okay?"

She opened her mouth to protest, thought better of it, and closed her lips, licking them before she nodded. "Okay."

Fuck. What a good girl.

"Get on, beautiful," I ordered after I tucked the tarp into my panniers and fired up the engine. "We don't want to linger here long."

Her eyes widened like she just remembered the Dirty Death MC and our whole reason for coming here.

As she slid behind me and wrapped her arms around my waist, it occurred to me that I never had a woman on the back of my bike until now. Some of my brothers weren't as picky about that shit as me, but I saw it as a statement—a declaration of my intention. No woman rode behind me unless I planned to claim her as mine. Hence the reason no one ever had.

Until now. Callie was quickly breaking all my rules.

Did I hate it? Fuck no.

It felt fucking right. Should have made me pause and consider the ramifications, but I didn't. I wanted her body as close to mine as possible, and if we had the time, I'd be fucking her on this bike too.

No reason to deny the truth. I fucking hungered for this girl.

We exited the garage and headed out, merging onto the highway and out of Henderson, riding toward Vegas. The gym Crow sent me the address for was located in a strip mall in a shady part of the city. Well, shit, all of Vegas was fucking shady, but this area was known for crime and the sex trade.

I didn't like bringing Callie, but it couldn't be helped. I wasn't leaving her outside or dropping her off. The only option remaining was to grasp her hand and lead her inside to the locker.

Once we found the gym and parked, I didn't give her a chance to refuse, clasping her fingers tightly as we walked inside the door. No one stopped or questioned me. That probably had to do with the fact that the staff were fucking against the counter when we walked in.

Shit. Vegas wasn't the city of sin. It was the cesspool of sex and the loss of inhibition. The stench of it saturated the air. My senses became overloaded with it as I fought my reaction.

My dick became engorged. Rigid, I resisted the urge to groan as tingles erupted along my shaft, spurring my lust. It had nothing to do with the couple on the counter or their moans.

No, this had everything to do with the girl beside me, who gasped but didn't stop watching as we walked by. She bit her plump lower lip, and I could swear I saw her thighs clench together once.

I scanned the lockers, finding the number I needed. I released Callie's hand long enough to dig out the key from the pocket of my cut, unlock the locker, and jump back as it began ticking.

No. Fucking. Way.

My protective instincts kicked in, and I threw my body in front of Callie, shielding her from whatever explosion would follow.

That motherfucking prick Undertaker would answer for this.

Shrapnel flew outward as I tackled her to the ground. My hand cradled the back of her hand as we landed on the hard ground. Above us, the sharp pieces of metal slammed into the lockers.

My heart raced as I cursed, pissed I didn't use more caution. I should have suspected that Undertaker would use this as a ruse. He wanted us dead. Message fucking received.

That motherfucker just escalated the war between our clubs.

He almost hurt Callie. That pissed me off as I looked into her eyes, searching them for any hint that she was hurt.

"You okay?" I asked, cradling the side of her face. "Fuck."

"I'm fine. Just a bit dazed."

Yeah, I didn't doubt it.

I hauled her up and into my arms as I stood, wrapping my arms around her back and rubbing it awkwardly. I sucked at this shit. Comforting a woman was new ground for me.

"Hawk."

"Yeah, love?"

"Can we go now?"

I snorted, lowering my chin to place a kiss on her forehead. Glancing into the locker, I noticed nothing had been in there but the explosive device that detonated when I opened the locker. "Yeah. We can leave."

Cautious, I led her back through the gym, noting that the couple at the front desk never moved, still getting it on as we rushed by them.

Fucking hell. Only in Vegas.

I REACHED FOR THE helmet on Callie's head, unbuckling the strap before lifting it off as she brushed her hair out of her eyes. The wind had kicked up, swirling sand in the air.

"I need to talk to Crow once we're inside. Will you be alright?"

"Sure." Her teeth nibbled on her bottom lip. A sign she felt anxious. "How long will that take?"

"I can't say for certain. I'm not leaving the chapel until we have a plan."

"Okay. I trust you, Hawk."

I didn't doubt it.

"C'mon, beautiful. I want to introduce you to the club."

Inside, the packed bar had come alive. My brothers settled around the leather sofas or the pool tables, shooting pocket billiards and slinging back shots. Club girls strutted through the crowd, hoping to snare one of them for the night. It struck me that I usually played that game and enjoyed flirting until I picked which one of them I wanted to fuck.

None of it interested me tonight.

I held Callie's hand tighter, pulling her against my side. The thought of her gaining attention irritated me. She wasn't a sweet butt or an easy piece of ass. No one would disrespect her or get the wrong idea because I planned to make it clear from the fucking start.

"Hawk!"

I didn't notice who called my name until Claw appeared. His drunk ass stumbled, one arm slung around a blonde named Josie. I'd fucked her at least twice in the last couple of months and hoped she kept her mouth shut.

"Hey, Hawk," she greeted, smiling with those bright red lips nearly all of my brothers had wrapped around their dick at one point or another. She could suck a golf ball through a hose but, for the first time, that shit disgusted me.

"Man, where you been?" Claw asked, squinting at me like he couldn't make his eyes open. Too damn high to do shit about it or care either.

Laughing, I shook my head. "Ridin'."

"Hi, Hawk."

Another soft, slightly higher-pitched voice called my name. The redhead it belonged to popped out her hip, giving Callie a bold perusal.

"Serenity."

Christ. I'd fucked her against every wall in the clubhouse two weeks ago. She loved sex out in the open and in front of anyone who wanted to watch.

Please don't say a fucking word to my woman.

"Where have ya been, Hawk, baby?"

Serenity's best friend and often sexual partner linked her arm through Jay's as they walked up to us. Tink winked as I tried to hold in a groan.

Goddamn. I was a fucking man whore. This proved it.

Never gave a fuck about it either until I saw the pink color dusting Callie's cheeks, and she released my hand. I guess it wasn't too hard to figure out these women had seen my dick on multiple occasions. Hell, I slept with some of them at the same time.

Jay just grinned, watching the drama unfold.

Asshole.

"Hawk!" Crow shouted, his voice drowning out the music. "We need to talk before church." His gaze fell on Callie, and he sighed. "The sooner, the better."

Well, shit. Pres wasn't happy with me.

"Be right there," I hollered back as he walked to his office carrying a bottle of Jack.

"Hey," I began, tilting Callie's chin so her eyes met mine. "I'll explain what's happening to Crow. Shouldn't be long."

"Fine."

Fuck. She was pissed, probably because of the club girls.

"Listen, my goddess. There ain't a single woman in this room who compares to you. You're right here." I tapped my head and my heart. "You feel me?"

She released a shaky breath. "Maybe."

I lowered my head, capturing her mouth in a sultry kiss that I purposely poured enough passion into to make those muffler bunnies back off. No room for doubt. Callie was mine.

A few whistles erupted, and some lewd comments followed.

I lifted my middle finger, flipping the room off.

Callie shook her head when we parted. "You're crazy."

"Only about you."

I reached into my cut, pulling out my keys. "Have a drink or whatever you want while you wait. You can go to my room too if you need a break from the party. It's the third door on the right on the second floor. Stairs are at the end of the hall."

She accepted the keys, dropping them into the purse she always wore, the strap resting across her chest from shoulder to hip. "I think I can manage."

Yeah, I knew she could.

"I'll look for Bree. We need to catch up."

Searching her eyes, I couldn't help feeling she was sent into my life for a reason. Maybe fate. Who knew?

But all I could think about as I walked away was how those gray eyes saw the real me, and she hadn't run yet.

TEN

GALLIE

OH NO, HE DIDN'T.

Hawk slept with every one of these women. I could sense their amusement as he cleared his throat, desperate for them to keep his secret. The thing was, women weren't stupid. We had intuition. Not to mention, we weren't blind either.

He was an idiot to think otherwise.

Flustered, I pulled my hand from his, gripping the strap of my purse. I wanted to be angry that he stuck his dick in every woman in this clubhouse, but it occurred to me that he had the right to do whatever he wanted. We weren't a couple. We just met. Why did I react like this after one night?

Because he's sexy and flirtatious, and he's the sweetest guy you've ever met.

I had been so focused on college and my career, then my sister's disappearance, that I hadn't dated anyone new since my freshman year. That was a hell of a dry spell.

The vibrator in my nightstand had gotten more action than I cared to admit.

I didn't expect Hawk to press his sensuous lips to mine in front of everyone. Or his mouth to linger, deepening that kiss until a soft growl worked its way up his throat. He took his time, savoring every second until we finally parted.

My cheeks heated, and my core clenched.

I called him crazy, and he didn't skip a beat, replying he was crazy only for me. Had we really only met a day ago? It seemed like I had known him for years.

How could my heart already begin to recognize him? Or long for his cocky smile and endless jokes?

Did I develop some whacked-out version of a nightingale effect? Had I fallen for my rescuer, the man who saved me and my sister? And he promised to keep protecting me without asking for anything in return. So selfless. Who would have thought the playboy biker was all heart?

"Callie!"

I jolted when I heard my name, searching the room until I found Bree. "Oh my God!" I squealed, rushing to my best friend. I wasn't kidding when I referred to her that way. We formed a bond over Sadie's disappearance, and I missed her over the last few weeks. "Where have you been?"

"It's a long story," she sighed, staring up at the handsome older biker who slid an arm around her waist, pulling her close. "This is Raven. He's, my uh," she faltered.

"I'm hers. That's the easiest way to say it," he laughed. His deep, sensual voice must drop panties all over this club. Not to mention his bald head, bulging muscles, and a salt-and-pepper beard. The definition of silver fox.

"I'm Callie." I reached out, shaking his hand. "You hurt her, and I'll find a way to make your life miserable."

A dark chuckle left Raven's lips. "Fiesty. You'll fit right in." He pressed a kiss to Bree's temple. "I'd never hurt my love."

Wow. I could tell he meant that. I wondered what happened to bring the two of them together.

Bree noticed my curiosity. "He was there for me in my lowest, darkest hour. Raven saved me."

"Well, he's a keeper then." Someday I'd ask her about it, but I could tell she seemed a little anxious. I didn't want to pry.

"Have you found Sadie yet?"

"No. That's why I'm here. Hawk is talking to Crow."

Raven lowered his head, landing a scorching kiss on Bree's lips. "I'll let you two catch up. Text if you need me, babygirl. I won't go far."

"I will."

Bree stuck her arm through mine and led me out of the bar, stopping in front of a door in the same hall where Crow and Hawk were having their meeting. She used a key to open it, gesturing for me to join her.

"I like this room because it's private. No one else can access it except for the officers. Raven made a copy of his key for me."

I noticed similar décor to the bar, including black leather furniture, dark wood, a giant 4k television mounted on the wall, a minibar, and a coffee table in the middle of the room with scuff marks, probably from multiple pairs of boots.

"It's comfy."

She walked to the bar. "Thirsty? I've got frozen margaritas."

"Yes, please." After all the stress I'd been under lately, a drink sounded perfect.

Bree joined me, handing over the margarita as I sipped from the salted rim. Delicious.

"So, have you learned anything new about Sadie?"

"Not really. Hawk seems sure Undertaker has my sister, and I'm inclined to believe him. I bet he's involved with all the missing girls. He probably blackmailed the mayor."

"That theory fits," she agreed. "Add in all the stuff we found in Elliot's safe, and I'd say he was trying to find a way to save his own ass."

"That sounds about right." I sighed, setting down my drink. "I hate not knowing if she's okay. That's the hardest part. I wish she could text me or find a way to get me a message."

"Aw, babe." Bree set her glass next to mine. "You need a hug."

"I really do," I blubbered.

She wrapped her arms around me as I sniffled. She hugged me as tight as my sister, and I fought back tears. When we separated, she picked up her drink, slinging half of it down. I noted it seemed different than mine. Non-alcoholic. I wondered if she skipped the liquor because of medical reasons. She said she wasn't feeling well when we spoke last.

"You know, I have to ask, what's going on with you and Hawk? He's never been so openly attached to one girl. I saw how he looked at you."

"Oh? What do you mean?"

"Literal hearts were pulsing from his eyeballs," she joked.

"You're silly," I laughed.

"Really. He was completely caught up in you. Didn't even like the club girls around. I could tell."

"That's probably because he's slept with all of them," I deadpanned, hating the jealousy in my voice. It was a ridiculous emotion, but I still felt it's sting.

She made a face. "Yeah. I believe so. I won't lie to you. But I think he's embarrassed by it. I've never seen him so uncomfortable."

Huh. That was interesting.

"I don't see why they had to be all over his dick when we walked in."

"To stake a claim. That lifestyle is cutthroat. Many of them want to be an ol' lady. They're hoping one of the guys grows attached." Bree shrugged. "I've seen it."

"I don't like it," I admitted. "It's weird to say that."

"Why? Because you haven't known each other long?"

"Well, yes."

"I thought the same thing about Raven, but the heart never lies. If you feel that connection, go for it. Why not? Even if it doesn't work out, you had fun in the process."

"Is this the same Bree from work? Did you head swap with someone else?" I joked.

"I know. I've been a bit stuffy in the past." She shrugged. "I'm learning to embrace my body and what I want. Raven is helping me through the process."

"I bet he is." I couldn't help laughing. "Good for you, Bree."

"Are you attracted to Hawk?"

"It's more complicated than that."

"No, it's not. Do you want to stay friends or see if there's more?"

"It really is a little more complicated." I told her about Hawk and how he went to prison for beating up Jed, saving my sister's life. "He saved me yesterday too. Took a bullet in his side because we were being chased by the Dirty Death MC. He might be a playboy, but he's also one of the best men I've ever met."

"It sounds like you already made your choice. You're just afraid to act on it."

Was that true? "Maybe."

"Listen. Let me tell you something that's going to be hard to hear. Stick with me, okay?"

I could never have imagined the horror that Bree experienced in the time we'd been apart. Kidnapped. Raped. My hand flew over my mouth, and I shook my head, tears spilling over as I listened, crying with her as she revealed what she had endured.

"So you see why I'm no longer living life by the rules. I want to be happy, Callie. And Raven makes me happy."

I reached for her hand, holding it in mine. "I'm so sorry that happened to you."

"It's hard. Sometimes I fight depression and nightmares, but I'm not alone. Raven would die for me. He almost did. I've never known a love like the one we feel for each other."

I swiped the tears from my cheeks. "I want to experience that too."

"Do you think Hawk is worth the risk?"

"You know, I do," I replied firmly. "I hate that he's slept with so many women, but that's not the man I see when I look into his eyes. I see a good man, outlaw or not."

She smiled, rising to her feet. "Then let's get you ready."

"For what?"

"Operation Seduce Hawk."

I giggled. Couldn't help it. The idea kind of excited me. "Alright. Give me a makeover and help me choose an outfit."

Her green eyes lit up like emeralds. "Yes!"

I let her drag me from the room, scooping up my margarita before we rushed into the hall, laughing at her enthusiasm.

HAWK

"WHAT DOES THIS GIRL mean to you, Hawk? Tell me why the fuck I would risk the lives of the men in this club."

From the minute I walked inside Crow's office, I couldn't sit still. I kept pacing, smoking my fourth cigarette during our discussion. My finger shook a little from the nicotine, but it didn't matter. Only Callie and Sadie did.

Well, fuck, the club did too. I wasn't choosing between the girls or the guys that had become family.

"Do you remember Sadie Withers?"

Crow sat back, pulling a smoke from the pack in his hand. He paused, tilting his head to the side. "The woman you went to prison for five years ago."

"The same one."

"What the fuck does that have to do with this?"

"Callie's last name is Withers."

Crow narrowed his eyes. "You sure?"

"Yeah. She's her sister. Bree and Callie worked together in the mayor's office. You know the shit they've been putting together about his corruption and criminal activity."

"Fuck," Crow cursed. "I didn't put it together until now."

"I didn't either at first. Not until Callie told me her sister's name. Then it all clicked." I already told Crow about being chased and laying low at the Powder Keg. Falcon filled him in about the gunshot wound to my side and how Marcus stepped up, providing a place for me to crash. We owed him. "I didn't intend to get involved again, but this shit is fucking happening. I have to help Sadie and Callie."

"You're not telling me everything. I can sense your Crow."

"You're never going to believe me."

"Stop fucking around and say it, Hawk."

"Christ. Okay, pres." I crushed the butt of my cigarette in the ashtray. "I think Callie is my, uh, mate."

"No shit?"

I rubbed the back of my neck. "Yeah. I can't stop thinking about her, and I don't want to fuck any of the club girls. Isn't that goddamn insane? I can't seem to walk around without a fucking hard-on, and it's all for Callie. I feel this overwhelming need to protect her, and I want to fucking rip those Dirty Death assholes apart for messing with her family. Fuck, pres, I—"

Crow held up a hand. "Yeah. You found your mate."

"How can you be sure?"

"Because that's how I felt with Bella. I would fucking kill to keep her safe. Just knowing she's in danger because of Undertaker and his bullshit is pissing me off. I'm agitated. I want to go home, fuck her, and keep her in my lap until this is all over. It's fucking anarchy in my brain."

I dropped into the chair in front of his desk. Having this confirmed, and hearing he experienced the same intense feelings, actually calmed me a little. "Wow. I guess the crow knows, huh?"

"Yeah, he fucking does. We can't sit on this. I'm calling church for noon. We'll figure out a plan and take it to vote."

"Appreciate that, pres."

"I need my ol' lady," he groaned.

Enough said. "I'll be claiming Callie now."

Crow shook his head with a laugh. "Don't be late to church."

"I won't," I promised, exiting the office, anxious to find Callie.

My head was full of all the shit I wanted to say to her, but it flew right out, wiped clean, as I stared at the goddess sitting on a stool at the bar.

Long bare legs, silky smooth under the dim lights, beckoned from across the room. I blocked out every noise, every other person in the vicinity. My hungry gaze swept over her trim waist, flared hips, deep cleavage, and bare shoulders. The tiny black dress on her body seemed painted on, revealing every creamy inch of her skin.

Fuck. Me.

Some sort of sound left my throat, and I couldn't say if I growled or ordered everyone from the room, or just declared my undying devotion. Maybe all three.

Callie sipped on a glass of wine, turning my way. "Hawk."

That sensual husky tone of voice sent ripples of lust straight to my cock. "My treasure," I whispered as I reached her, unable to keep my hands from her body. I didn't even want to kiss her yet, just stare at the sensual, gorgeous woman I wanted to be mine.

Before my lips had a chance to meet hers, I slid her closer, wrapping my hands around the back of her thighs. In one swift movement, I had her legs around my waist, growling when she crossed her ankles behind my back.

Two small hands slid across my stomach, gliding up my chest, and slowly began to stroke the back of my head and neck. A needy, feral noise escaped my mouth. I had her ass in my palms, gripping the thick, juicy globes as I realized she only wore a thong. Nothing prevented me from slipping it aside and driving deep inside her, right here, right now.

I was so fucking tempted.

But fucking her in front of the club wasn't what I wanted. Not with Callie. I didn't want any of my brothers to see the pussy I was claiming for myself. For once, I wanted something pure, untainted by dozens of other men. Instinctually, I knew Callie hadn't been with many partners. That excited me.

"Do you have any idea how fucking sexy and beautiful you are? How much I can't wait to make you mine?"

ELEVEN

HAWK

"**D**O YOU HAVE ANY idea how fucking sexy and beautiful you are? How much I can't wait to make you mine?"

Callie shook her head. "No. I want you to show me."

With her cunt pressed flush against my hard and ready cock, I already have trouble convincing myself that I shouldn't lay her down on one of the pool tables and feast on her pussy. I wanted to taste her, memorize her moans and breathy sighs. I needed to know how she felt when I was inside her and watch her face as she came.

We needed to get to my room. Fast.

I gripped her body tight and rushed down the hall, ignoring all the fuckers making comments that didn't register in my head. I was too full of the woman in my arms to give a shit.

At my door, I chuckled when Callie handed over my keys. Her impatience matched mine.

Once inside, I shut the door and locked it, slowly backing away as I moved toward my bed.

Unable to deny myself any longer, my lips latched onto her neck, tugging her head back as I licked, sucked, and devoured the skin. She tasted like fucking heaven. As close as a man like me could ever get. I followed a trail up to her ear with open-mouthed kisses, leaving a wet pathway behind. My teeth nipped at her earlobe.

"Fuck, Callie. Do you have any idea what I want to do with you?"

A gasp left her lips as I attacked the other side of her neck, falling onto my bed as I rolled my hips into the apex of her thighs. I wanted her to enjoy this. To come so hard she saw stars—more than once.

I pulled back long enough to rip off my cut and fling it toward the headboard. My T-shirt followed.

Callie reached for the hem of her dress, already bunched at her waist. I helped lift it, carefully revealing the matching bra to her thong.

Goddamn. Bright fucking red with lace. Half of the material was see-through, exposing her nipples. I tugged the fabric down, popping one breast out as I lowered my head and slid my tongue over the bud, teasing and rolling it as a soft moan fell from her lips.

"I need this off."

Helping her sit up, I unsnapped the clasps, pulling the straps down her arms and away from her body. There are tits. And then there are beautiful fucking tits a man can't get enough of. She had the latter.

I couldn't help dividing my attention between them, feeling the hardened pebbles underneath my tongue. Cupping the soft swells that overfilled my palm, I grazed my thumb over the nipples, enjoying the way her hips began to tilt toward me.

Her arousal did wicked things to my brain.

Desire flared between us as I snapped my hips, desperate to make contact with her pussy. I needed to feel her yielding to me as she sucked me in. My head buzzed with lust and my cock throbbed in response.

Rising, I finally allowed my lips to meet hers, twisting my tongue as I slipped through the seam, devouring her like a man possessed. I couldn't say how long the kiss lasted, but I nipped at her bottom lip before resuming my kisses down her neck, across her collarbone, and lower.

Fuck. That incredible scent of hers washed over me.

As I licked at her skin, tasting her, I knew I could never get enough.

Making my way down her body, I grazed my fingertips over her bare thighs, inching toward her center. Leaning in, I dropped kisses above her mound, watching her reaction.

"Have you ever had a man starving to devour your pretty cunt?"

She shook her head, panting as she watched me hook my fingers in the silk and gently slide it downward. I didn't pull it all the way off, leaving the material dangling from one leg as I pushed it up and out, exposing her pussy.

It felt like I had waited centuries to see her, touch her. Personally, I wasn't a boob guy. Tits were great, but I loved a woman's ass, her curves, and most of all, pussy. I loved sticking my tongue through her folds, lapping her core, and tasting her natural essence. My mouth watered at the thought of diving in and watching her squirm.

Dipping down, I placed one hand on her stomach, holding her in place. Staring at the bare pink paradise in front of me, I adjusted my dick. My jeans constricted too much.

She sucked in a breath as I flicked out my tongue, giving her clit a little teasing caress. After a dark chuckle, I dove in, licking and sucking, lapping at her entrance as I spread her open. So fucking wet and glistening.

"Oh, God. Yes, Hawk," she groaned as I inserted a finger. Encouraged by the way her hips began pumping, I added another, still nibbling on her swollen clit.

Fuck me. The noises coming from her mouth turned me the fuck on. I felt her inner walls slicken, her body preparing to come.

"Hawk. I need you. Please."

"What do you need?" I asked, gliding my fingers in and out faster. "Tell me. Describe it."

"I need your cock inside me," she panted.

"I'm going to use a condom this time, sweetling, but I want you to know I won't be in the future. I want to feel you bare. Nothing separating us from the pleasure, okay?"

"What if I want to skip it now?"

I didn't think she would agree to that because of all the other women I'd been with recently.

"We stick to this for now."

She nodded, her gaze falling on my dick. I stripped as she watched, loving how she seemed engrossed in my every movement and kicked off my boots. I reached inside my jeans, pulled out a rubber, and ripped the package open, sheathing the shaft. It wasn't my favorite, but I wouldn't risk it until I knew I was clean.

I gripped my cock, easing it toward her pussy, relieved when I saw how wet she had become. Coating the tip in her juices, I slid back and forth, grinning at her as she moaned.

"You're teasing me."

"I'm making sure you want this."

"Oh, I do. Fuck me, Hawk. Now."

I pressed inside a couple of inches, slowly filling her. My hips began to pump, driving me deeper as I slid out slow, then fast in, repeating that until I had bottomed out, slapping my balls against her ass.

Fuck. "You feel so damn good."

"Oh, God, Hawk. So do you."

"Yeah?"

"Yes!"

"Fuck. You're so tight."

I picked up the pace, finding a steady rhythm with every thrust, so fucking blissed out that I had to stop myself from coming too early. My fingers slid between her legs, strumming her clit as Callie's thighs began to shake.

"I'm going to come."

She barely said the words before her body tensed, then released, her pussy spasming around my cock. "Hawk!"

Her hips bucked, and her movements grew erratic as I rode out her orgasm, knowing I wasn't far behind. My lower body began to move at an impossible rate, and I knew I was digging my fingers into her ass as I chased that high only sex could offer. The difference this time was the woman in my arms.

My gaze locked on hers as I lost the battle, tipping over the edge as I grunted, spilling myself inside her. The condom would prevent any leak, but I thought of Callie becoming pregnant and knew it would happen someday. That thought made me want to go another round and I would before the night was over.

My limp body rolled to the side after I pulled out, reaching down to rid my dick of the condom. I hopped up, dropping it into the trash before joining Callie on the bed.

She looked tired but relaxed. "That was amazing."

"Fuck yeah, it was." I leaned over and kissed her, then rolled onto my back, drawing her into my embrace.

Neither of us spoke for several long minutes, enjoying the peace amidst the storm brewing outside these walls.

"I'm glad we met," she whispered, cutting through the silence.

"I'm fucking lucky, beautiful. I'll be thankful every day that you're with me."

"You're too sweet," she yawned.

"Rest, Callie. I'm not going anywhere."

Neither of us moved the entire night.

Waking with a woman in my arms was a new experience. One I never cared about before now to explore.

Callie's head rested over my heart, and I lazily swept my fingers over her spine, caressing her skin. How did she keep it so soft? And was that perfume or body spray that hinted at citrus and wildflowers? Because it was fast becoming a scent that I couldn't live without.

Me. The guy who never remembered the name of the girl he fucked the night before or mixed up the names of sweet butts in the past. The one who didn't believe in romance. I smirked as I thought about Callie and a date. The fact that I considered it all proved I wasn't fucking around.

I could hardly wrap my head around it.

My phone buzzed as I reached for it and checked the time, cursing when I realized it was nearly noon.

Shit! I didn't want to leave Callie but I couldn't miss church. It was too important.

Pushing her hair aside, I kissed her forehead. "Sweetling, I need to leave. It's almost noon."

She mumbled something I couldn't make out.

"Crow is waiting for me to start church."

Her eyes fluttered. "Okay."

"Don't leave. I'll find you when it's over."

"Mm-hmm."

Heading to the bathroom, I took a piss and dressed, stopping to gaze at the gorgeous woman in my bed.

I pulled up the covers, tucked her in, and smiled as I left my room, closing the door behind me.

Crow stared me down as I entered the chapel, the last to arrive. "Sleep well, princess?"

A few of my brothers snickered.

"Yeah, yeah. I'm here, pres."

He picked up the gavel, slamming it down as he called the meeting to order.

"We all know what this shit is about. Fucking Undertaker and his club. They shot Hawk and nearly injured Callie. This vendetta will continue until he gets what he wants. He isn't going to stop."

"No, he's not," I agreed. "We need to make a move. Show him we're not gonna back down from this fight."

Jay slammed a fist down on the table. "I'm tired of hearing about Undertaker's bullshit."

"He sent his fucking guys to the hospital to finish me off," Raven reminded us. "They wanted to take Bree and assault her all over again. If anyone wants that motherfucker to pay, it's me." He didn't add that Chronos had assaulted Bree for eight days before Raven rescued her because Undertaker ordered it. The fucking bastard.

"You have that right," Crow agreed. "So does Hawk."

I cleared my throat. "For lots of reasons. Crow sent me to the gym with the key Undertaker left us. He fucking put a bomb in the locker at the gym. I had to dive for the fucking floor to avoid the metal fragments. Callie almost got hurt."

"Christ," Crow muttered.

"That's not all. Sadie Withers has a sister named Callie."

I let that sink in.

"My Callie."

"Are you sayin' the chick you helped out and went to jail for is the missing girl on the news?"

"Yeah. Callie and Bree were working together to figure out what happened to Sadie. I think Undertaker has her."

Cuckoo whistled. "Damn, bro. How do you get mixed up in this shit?" He snorted, shaking his head. "Okay. So you feel you gotta help the girls out, right?"

"That's the gist."

"All the women are in danger until the DDMC and Undertaker are dealt with," Crow announced. "I need to hear what you want to do about it."

The surge of protectiveness I felt over Callie made me tense up. "I won't wait around for Undertaker to attack again. We've sat too long. I vote we bring the crows."

Crow scrubbed a hand down his face. "We need to remember that Undertaker is like us. He's not a crow, but he's got an animal. Something mean. It's not a regular wolf."

"No," Claw agreed. "It's not. I've seen wolves. They're deadly, but not like this."

"So, is he the only one? Or do they all have that ability? Because I haven't sensed it," Raven added.

"We don't know," Crow admitted.

Raven shook his head. "We need to find out first. Going in blind is foolish."

"Fuck," I cursed. "Okay."

Crow ticked his chin at Jay and Claw. "Check it out. Sneak close to the DDMC lair and let me know what you find."

"You got it, pres."

"Eagle Eye? What have you been able to dig up?"

Eagle Eye paused typing on his laptop. He never said much until someone spoke to him directly.

"Lots about the Dirty Death financials. They're dealing with a few high rollers in Vegas with deep pockets. Business is good for them. Too good."

"What the fuck does that mean?"

"Well, pres, it's fake as shit. Their books aren't real records. The accountant is terrible at it. I'm digging into several paper trails now."

"Find something we can use as leverage."

"Will do, pres."

Crow pounded a fist on the table. "Just so we're all clear, Undertaker will pay for what he's done. I need him to suffer for taking my pops." He sneered, holding onto his anger but it was a struggle. "Everyone be fucking ready when this goes down."

Heads nodded around the room.

"Anything else?" Crow asked, his gaze bouncing around each of us. "No? Then church is fucking over."

No one blamed Crow for feeling the way he did. Undertaker was responsible for his father Rook's death. We lost our president too fucking early and it nearly destroyed the club. We all had vengeance on our minds and wouldn't rest until we got the justice the Devil's Murder needed.

TWELVE

CALLIE

"Y ou're going where tomorrow?" Hawk asked, cracking his neck, clearly agitated at my words.

"Work. I have to go so the mayor doesn't get suspicious."

He snorted. "That should be the last of your worries."

"Well, it's not. I still don't know where my sister is, even if Undertaker has her. You said I'm being watched. If that's true, I need to pretend like nothing has changed."

He sighed. "I don't like it, and I don't fucking trust the mayor. He's involved in some dangerous shit. It doesn't make sense to put you in harm's way by letting you return to that job."

"You're being overprotective and not thinking rationally."

"Callie. Please reconsider this, beautiful."

"What if something happens to my sister because I don't follow my routine? I couldn't live with that."

He reached for my jaw, tilting my head up. "Babe. The mayor doesn't have any control over what happens to your sister. I'm certain of that."

"But I'm not convinced."

"Okay," he relented. "But I'll be there after your shift ends."

"Thank you." I lifted on my toes, trying to reach his mouth for a kiss, when his arms slid around me, hauling me upward.

"Promise me you'll keep in touch all day, so I don't fucking stress about this."

He murmured the words against my lips.

I closed the tiny bit of space between us, initiating a kiss as he groaned, loving how Hawk's hands squeezed my ass. He was the type of guy easily turned on by affection, but it was more than that. With me, he became singularly focused. No other woman mattered.

After what I learned about his past, it proved he wasn't just using me for sex. He could have that whenever he wanted with any of those club girls, but he wanted *me*. Just me.

"If you're returning to work tomorrow, I get you today. All fucking day."

"Alright. What do you want to do?"

He stole another kiss, then wiggled his eyebrows. "Babe, keeping you in bed sounds perfect."

"The whole day?"

He thought about it. A slow grin spread his lips wide. "Is there a limit on how many times I can make you come?"

Nope.

He carried me across the clubhouse, nibbling on my neck most of the way. By the time we entered the room, I was ready to rip off his clothes.

A dark laugh tumbled from his lips as he dropped me on the bed, tugging at my clothes. We'd taken it slow last night.

For our first time together, it was perfect. Hawk's patience and his desire to savor our joining meant the world to me. It wasn't a quick, meaningless fuck.

But now? Hard and fast was all I wanted.

Both of us were naked fast. I reached for his cock, slowly working my hand up and down the shaft. Hawk's eyes partially closed, half-lidded as he cursed, moving his hips as he increased the friction.

There was something incredibly sensual and erotic about watching his facial expressions and noticing the increased rate of his breaths. The way that he responded to me, capturing my mouth as I continued to stroke him, made me grow wetter. The palm of his hand began to caress my hip, moving lower to glide across my thigh.

My legs opened wide to give him access.

"So fucking beautiful. I love how soft and wet you are, how ready you are for me to fuck you."

Two of his fingers slid between my folds, dipping into my pussy, coating his fingers in the slick, and then rising to press down on my clit. He began to rub tiny circles into the nubbin as I gave a little twist of my wrist and tightened my grip on his cock.

"Fuck. Do that again."

I twisted again, rubbing my thumb over the crown.

"Jesus. Fuck. I need inside you," he growled.

I guess I pushed him over the edge as I smiled, and he lined up his cock, pushing inside me as I gasped. His thrusts were fast and erratic, pumping hard as he placed one hand on the bed for leverage. The other grasped my jaw as he stared into my eyes.

"You and me, this is real." *Thrust.* "I can't get enough of you." *Another thrust.* "You feel so fucking good. So goddamn perfect."

117

His hips rolled, punching forward as he glided in and out of me, driving my bottom into the mattress. "You were made for me."

Yeah, I was beginning to believe that too.

His mouth covered mine in a wet, open-mouthed, hungry kiss as the headboard slammed into the wall. The slap of flesh on flesh filled the room.

"You hear that? That's me fucking you, gorgeous."

God, I loved the way he talked dirty to me.

I fell apart only a minute later, convulsing around him as my body exploded in euphoria, crying out his name as my nails clawed at his biceps.

"Hawk. Oh, God. Hawk!"

"That's it. Come, babe. You're soaking me and the sheets. So fucking addicting. I love feeling you squirt like this."

His eyes almost rolled back into his head as he pounded into me, jerking his hips as he found his release. I felt him spurting, coating the inside of my pussy, and I clutched him against my chest. Never in my life did I feel such a fierce attraction and completeness as I did with Hawk.

Could you find your forever in only a single moment of bliss?

Hawk stayed buried inside me as he stilled, lowering to his forearms while continuing to kiss me, devouring my lips. He nipped my bottom lip, tugging on it lightly before releasing it. The way he looked at me as if I had become his whole world sent shivers down my spine.

Falling in love with someone you just met seemed like a fairytale. Prince Charming didn't exist. Neither did a perfect relationship. But Hawk couldn't hide how he felt about me, and I couldn't deny that my heart was already falling for him.

"I came inside you, Callie." He seemed concerned. "I should have given you a choice."

"I wanted it," I assured him.

"You on birth control?"

"I guess we should have discussed this earlier, but no. I've not been sexually active for years. It didn't seem necessary."

His mouth swooped down in a wild, passionate kiss. "That was fucking sexy to hear."

"Not if you knock me up," I joked.

"Maybe not yet, but someday, when we're ready, I want to fuck you until you are."

Oh, wow. He was serious. "Um, okay."

Okay? Really? I thought about it, waiting to feel anything wrong about it, and I didn't.

"Goddamn. I'm so fucking lucky. I love that no other guy has been with you that long."

He kissed me again, pulling out as he rose from the bed. I wondered what he was doing in the bathroom when he returned with a warm wet washcloth to clean me up.

We spent the afternoon talking. His fingers interlaced with mine as I sat on his lap, and we shared an intimate moment I would remember for a long time into the future.

Hawk surprised me later that night when he returned with a suitcase of my clothes and a bag full of my makeup and other necessities. "I knew you needed these." He cleared his throat. "I hope you'll be staying with me while we figure all this shit out."

"I am," I promised.

His shoulders relaxed. "Good."

The following morning, I showered and dressed for work, noting Hawk's sullen expression.

"Hey. It'll be fine. Besides, I'm sure you have things to do."

"Yeah," he admitted reluctantly.

"Follow me there. I like knowing you're behind me."

"Shit," he joked. "I will be later, for sure."

His caution and worry were sweet. I understood his reasons for it, but I had to live my life too. We needed to be able to compromise and accept the differences in our lives. I already knew he was a biker and outlaw. He'd have to learn about me too.

I parked in the garage designated for city employees a little before eight a.m., blowing Hawk a kiss as he sat on his motorcycle, waving before I entered the building.

Most of the morning sped by with all the work piled up from an intern who quit. I spent hours catching up and finally took a break. As I sipped on coffee, I swiped across the screen of my cell. Hawk had sent a message every hour.

How adorably stalker.

I texted back, assuring him I was fine, just busy.

The door to the break room opened, and Elliot walked inside. I hadn't seen him in so long it was almost shocking to find his debonair but wicked smile settled on me. He didn't stop at the vending machines or fridge, walking right up to my table.

"Callie. How have you been?"

"Great. Thanks."

His predatory, creepy grin popped a dimple on his left cheek. "That's wonderful to hear. We missed you the other night."

"Oh?"

"I had cocktails with a mutual friend. He mentioned something interesting."

I couldn't imagine what mutual friend we would have together. "Is it a secret?"

"No, actually." Cue the narcissistic smile. "You have the same last name as an intimate colleague of mine. Her name is Sadie. Sadie Withers."

Oh, no.

Shit. Shit. Shit!

Blinking, I stared into his face, and the knowing grin that widened the longer I kept silent. My face felt hot as a flush crept up my neck and into my cheeks. "Oh really?"

"What a coincidence. Don't you think?"

Nope.

"I guess that happens a lot," I mused, trying not to freak out.

"Perhaps." He strolled past the table, stopped, and brushed his fingertips over my shoulder. "You do resemble one another. Such pretty," he paused, "dolls."

Oh my God! He knew. Elliot Goodman knew Sadie was my sister!

I sucked in a breath, refusing to answer him, but I didn't have to because I already gave it away by my reaction.

"I've scheduled a meeting for five p.m. I'll need your services, Callie. Don't be late."

He straightened his tie, winked, and left the break room.

Only once he left did I stand, rushing to the sink to rinse out my coffee mug. I couldn't stay here, and I definitely couldn't show up at that meeting. If it was a meeting.

The mayor wouldn't get his chance to blackmail or use me.

I wanted to text Hawk but didn't dare until I left the building. Walking back to my office, I typed a quick correspondence to the mayor and shut down my computer. I wouldn't send it until after I sat in my car. I reached for my purse and rushed into the hall, avoiding conversation with any of the staff. If I needed to take sick time, I didn't need permission. I just had to let Elliot know I wasn't feeling well.

Outside the building, I sucked in fresh air, trying to calm my anxious heart. I nearly ran to my car, throwing my purse inside as I sat behind the wheel. My fingers shook as I started it, pushed down the locks, and logged into my work email.

I found the request for sick time in my draft folder and sent it to Elliot.

This was a fucking disaster. Why did I think it would be safe to come back here?

I scrolled through my contacts and dialed Agent Phillips, but his number went to voicemail like it had every day for weeks.

Full-blown panic threatened to consume me, but I forced myself to focus. Backing out of the parking space, I headed toward the garage exit.

There, across the street, smoking as he leaned against his bike, stood Hawk. I realized he probably spent most of the day there, waiting for me to leave. Bet he thought it would happen sooner, but it didn't matter now.

As soon as I saw him, a sob escaped my chest.

He noticed. His jaw clenched as he flicked the cigarette to the ground. It bounced, sparking as it hit the asphalt.

He tapped his chest over his heart and ticked his head in the direction of the Roost, his club's location.

I nodded, merged onto the street, and gripped the steering wheel as I drove.

The rumble of Hawk's bike alerted me to his presence a few seconds before I saw him appear in my rearview mirror.

I couldn't help the tears that formed as I blinked them back. Only two people were there for me when I needed them most in my life. One was missing, kidnapped by a monster. Riding on an iron beast, the other would follow me into hell. A dark knight and savior. The man who had claimed my heart.

UNDERTAKER

I WAS BORED. WHEN I grew bored, it spelled disaster.

The gun in my hand spun around as I twirled it, knowing I loaded it earlier and was itching for a reason to use it. Maybe I could sense the change coming in the air. My body grew restless, and even fucking didn't calm the beast.

He wanted blood. Carnage. A fresh kill.

Excess energy slid over my body and filled it, begging me to shift. I could go on a run. Hell, most of my club brothers would love it. They ached for the freedom of the beast as I did.

Of course, my animal was different. Always had been.

I was the alpha, and by process of elimination, I also became the president of the Dirty Death MC. Wolves were pack animals, and the life of a biker easily fit into our mentality. My father had been a wolf shifter, and his before him. But none had done what I did to ensure I became the strongest alpha.

The vargulf could only be controlled by an alpha. No other possessed the will or power to do it. The legend of the vargulf had been passed down for generations. Rumors of my family controlling the wild beast circulated among my brothers.

The Dirty Death MC was formed as a way to keep our lives hidden from the public, allowing our pack to thrive and grow. My lineage always ruled as president. We killed to ensure it, destroying all opposition. Other alphas were eliminated or sent into exile.

But in order to take on the vargulf, a member of my family had to kill an innocent, leave the body and organs without feasting, and force the shift under a moon that wasn't full. Every generation, a new vargulf emerged. Each completed the initiation to become the monster. As far as we knew, only one could exist at a time.

Ten years ago, I slaughtered my younger sibling to become the vargulf. She was only eight years old.

My lip twisted in a snarl as I pushed from my chair, leaving the bar where I'd been drinking since dawn. The wolf's metabolism burned off the liquor faster than I could consume it—one of the few things I hated about what I became.

When my mood was this foul, only Sadie calmed me.

I found her locked in her room, reading a book as she lounged on the balcony. I'd entered without permission, but that was nothing new.

"Sadie," I growled, overwhelmed with her scent. Clean rain. Fresh wildflowers. A hint of spice.

My cock swelled, engorged within a few seconds. "Come to me."

She set down the book and entered the bedroom, closing the sliding glass door behind her. "Hello, Undertaker."

I'd given her the best room in the compound. The balcony overlooked Lake Tahoe and the Sierra Nevada Mountains. I spoiled her and indulged her because I needed a mate.

The vargulf wanted to breed.

"Lay down on your back and show me your pussy."

"As you wish."

Sadie's hips mesmerized me. She had childbearing hips. The kind that would bear my children without worrying about miscarriage. A sturdy frame and curves in all the right places.

She stripped naked, laying her clothes on the bed. Then, taunting me as she usually did, she climbed onto the mattress on all fours. Her ass jiggled as she turned, flopped onto her back, and opened her legs.

"Wider."

I snapped the button on my jeans and released my cock, gripping it hard as I began to pump the length from base to tip.

"Touch yourself. I want to see your face as you come."

She never denied me.

With every dip of her fingers into her wet, juicy cunt, I stroked faster, harder. A grunt left my lips as I felt my orgasm build.

Sadie's hips began to move, her body responding to the lust unleashed freely between us. I had no illusion she did this for me. She obeyed because she was my prisoner.

But that would change soon.

I approached the bed, watching her beautiful face as she escaped me, lost in her thoughts and erotic fantasies. Soon, she wouldn't be able to do that. I wouldn't let her focus on anyone or anything but me.

My large hand landed on the mattress next to her head. I got as close as I could, still pumping up and down my cock. When her mouth opened, and she let out a moan, I watched her body convulse through her orgasm, joining her. Cum exploded from the tip of my swollen cock, coating her generous breasts, flat stomach, and then lower. I kept leaking fluid, excited as I hit the entrance to her pussy, hoping I managed to get some inside her.

Lowering to my knees, I shoved my head into her cunt, feasting on the combination of our fluids. I lapped at her with my thick, rough tongue, spearing it inside her until she couldn't resist playing with her clit, coming a second time as I ate up every drop.

"You are mine," I growled.

"You promised."

"I never touched you. Only my tongue. I'll use it anytime I wish."

She gasped, unable to hide the fear in her eyes.

Good. She understood I would claim and mate her soon. I needed a reason to keep her from resisting. Something she couldn't fight.

If I wanted Sadie to cooperate, there was only one way to ensure it. I licked the last of her essence and swallowed it down my throat, a slow smile working its way across my mouth.

Callie Withers. Sadie's sister.

My wild card.

THIRTEEN

HAWK

As soon as the gate shut behind us and we both parked, I hopped off my bike. Callie opened the door, flinging it open as I reached for the handle. All I cared about was comforting her. The terrified, worried expression on her face didn't disappear even after I kissed her.

Caw...caw.

The crow. He sensed the danger, agitated by Callie's fear.

His round body dropped from the sky, landing at my feet. Ruffling his feather, he began squawking, berating me for letting her leave.

Fucking crazy bird.

"Christ. Leave it be," I grumbled, scooping under Callie's legs and lifting her. "I've got you, my treasure. Let's get inside."

I still heard the crow complaining as I walked inside the Roost, annoyed but also amused as I set Callie down on a pool table, moving between her thighs as I cradled her face.

"Tell me what happened."

The room silenced as the conversations in the bar ceased. Everyone listened to Callie as she began to speak.

"The mayor," she began, breathing hard as her body shook.

"Hey," I replied softly, brushing her lips with a kiss. "Breathe for me, okay?"

Callie sucked in air, taking a minute to collect herself. "He came into the break room while I was there."

"Did he threaten you?" I growled.

She gave me an exasperated look as Crow yelled for me to shut the fuck up.

Damn.

"He said Sadie and I shared the same last name, and we were both pretty dolls." She shook her head. "That was intentional. He wanted me to know he found out the truth."

My hands balled into fists. I wouldn't lose my shit. Not in front of Callie. "What else?"

"Elliot ordered me to be at his meeting tonight. He said he needed my services and not to be late."

The fuck?

"What time?" Crow asked, joining us.

"Five p.m."

Crow nodded, ticking his head at Raven. The VP followed him out of the bar and down the hall to Crow's office.

"You won't be going," I snapped, struggling to remain calm. If I got too agitated, the crow would take over. Nobody wanted me to unleash him until it was time.

"Hawk," Callie whispered, brushing her fingers along my jaw. "I love that you're my dark champion and protector, but you need to chill."

Several of my brothers laughed. Fuckers.

"I'm terrified of what this conversation meant for Sadie. If I don't show up to that meeting, she could die. It's not an option."

My entire body stiffened. "No fucking way."

"You don't get to make that decision. Not alone. This is my life. My choice. My fucking sister."

She blinked as my hands wrapped around her body, and I buried my face in her neck. "I can't lose you when I just found you."

"That's why I won't be showing up alone."

Fuck. "Damn straight. I'm standing right by your side. Try to get rid of me. Not gonna happen."

"I was hoping you would say that because I'm going to ask you to let me arrive alone. There's no way Elliot will meet with me if you're growling like a bear and ready to rip him apart."

"She knows you too well already," Cuckoo joked.

I flipped him off, dismissing him as I caught the werewolf mask he wore, the mouth cut open wider as he chewed on a string of red licorice. "Why the fuck are you wearing that?"

"I appreciate the irony."

"You're fucking nuts."

"Everyone keeps sayin' that, but I don't see the problem." Cuckoo shrugged. "I'm gonna make some popcorn for the shit show about to go down. Anyone want some?"

He was referring to me and the fucking tantrum I was about to throw because Callie wanted to meet the mayor without me.

My brothers opened their wallets, slapping down twenties on the pool table. I knew what the assholes were doing, taking bets on my failure. They didn't doubt that Callie would get her way.

"Fuck all of you," I grumbled, but I didn't mean it.

"Don't be so sensitive, Hawk."

Claw could kiss my ass, and I told him that.

His chuckle irritated me. Wait until he found his mate. He would be the biggest asshole around.

Carrion pushed off the wall across from us, leaving the shadows where he liked to observe everything. "Check your phone, Callie."

"Why?" she asked, picking it up only to jolt when it vibrated with an incoming text.

"Tell him yes," Carrion added.

She stared at the screen, swiping across to read the message. "Okay." I saw her type a response, concerned when she bit her lip. "You sure that was the right thing to do?"

Carrion's eyes fluttered, rolling white a few seconds before he blinked. His vision returned to normal. "Yes." He turned to me. "Accept it, or you place her in irreversible danger."

My stomach churned. A headache formed behind my eyes as I imagined all the different ways this shit could go wrong.

Before I could reply to Carrion, he left the Roost. I heard his bike roar to life and knew wherever he went, it was vital.

Fuck. I hated when he acted cryptic like that.

"Elliot asked me to meet him at his favorite casino and to wear a black cocktail dress." Callie inhaled a shuddering breath. "He said he'd have a dozen red roses waiting and a gift."

I could feel her body trembling. "Don't be scared. I won't let anything happen to you."

"That's the same thing he did with all the missing girls, including Sadie. I'll end up wherever Sadie is." She sighed, her body relaxing. Her gaze shot to me. "If I want to find my sister, this is the only way."

Not gonna fucking happen. "Fuck, Callie."

"It's okay. I can do this."

"No. There has to be another way," I argued.

Callie shook her head. "You can't save everyone, Hawk."

That didn't matter to me anymore. Just the club and my brothers and their families and Callie and Sadie—

Fuck. I did want to save everyone.

"You're so amazing. The best guy I've ever met." Her lips met mine, and I savored the kiss, tasting her on my lips as she leaned back. "I don't know what happened to you, but I know it was rough."

I didn't hesitate to tell her. Nothing about my life was a secret anymore. "My father was an abusive prick. He liked to use me as a punching bag. When he wasn't hitting my mother, his aggression turned on me."

"Oh, Hawk. I'm so sorry."

"He killed her, sweetling. That motherfucker took my mother from me."

"That's why you hold on so tight to the club and now, to me."

"Yes." Damn. She could be a shrink. How did she figure all this out about me? Was I that transparent?

"I love that it's made you such a caring, protective man, but you can't control everything. Sometimes you have to surrender to the will of fate."

"Fate fucked me over, babe."

"No," she smiled. "Fate brought us together. Five years ago, to be exact, planting roots that would grow into the connection we've made over the last few days."

Wow. That was some intense shit right there.

"Okay," I finally agreed. "Let's do this."

Three hours later, Callie emerged from Bree's room, dressed in a tight, knee-length dress that shimmered like black pearls under the lights. She was so fucking beautiful it stole the breath from my chest. I floundered, choking, sucking air into my aching lungs.

"You like it?"

"I've never seen anyone look more gorgeous in my life."

Callie beamed a smile that made my heart flutter in response.

I fucking loved her. That goddamn fast. Boom. It hit me like a strike of lightning. I never stood a chance.

"You own my heart," I managed to say, nearly cringing from the sappy, romantic words spilling from my mouth that I would never have believed possible a month ago.

"And you own mine." Her soft, glossy lips collided with my own as I groaned, wishing I could take her into my room and prove every word I said was true.

It would have to wait.

"I'm driving you in one of our company SUVs. The windows are tinted, and no one will be able to see who's inside with you."

She nodded. "Perfect."

"You good? No worries?"

She shook her head, far braver than I felt. My skin itched as I fought the urge to let the crow free. Outside, I felt his restless energy and fury waging war, close to breaking down the barriers in place to keep the shift from happening.

My crow wasn't like my brothers. Like Carrion, I had experiences that altered our bond. We had a connection as strong as anyone else but also far more complex.

I didn't need to worry about that tonight. Concentrating on my woman, the one I planned to make my ol' lady, I led her from the Roost to the SUV. Sliding in beside her, I held her hand the entire ride.

We arrived at the casino with five minutes to spare.

After a kiss, I watched her leave the SUV and enter the building. Every instinct inside me screamed to follow her, but I trusted Carrion. He said nothing would happen. I believed him. In the past, I doubted, but not after his resurrection. When Falcon brought him back, his visions became intense, helping the club often.

Texting Callie, I waited for a response.

She didn't know it, but I brought her phone to Eagle Eye when she slept last night and asked him to hack it, enabling me to track her if anything happened.

Maybe that was bullshit, but I didn't feel guilty about it. Not with the Dirty Death, their attacks, or Undertaker and his vendetta. And then there was the fucking mayor and his hard-on for Callie and Sadie.

I pulled up the app on my phone, finding my woman's location. From what I could tell as I exited the vehicle, she waited at the bar for Elliot. Cocksucker better not touch her.

Claw and Raven flanked me. We left our cuts inside with Jay since he drove, hoping no one recognized us. So far, so good.

I made my way through the rows of slot machines, ignoring all the bells and flashing lights, the whirring of spinning reels, and the loud chimes. It took a minute to spot the bar, but I found it, hanging back as I searched for Callie.

My phone began beeping, letting me know she was close and on the move. Maybe she had to use the ladies' room or something.

Minutes ticked by as the beeping continued, but the app never showed her leaving the building. How the hell could she walk in circles, and I kept missing her?

Something wasn't right.

The beeping stopped as the dot on my screen vanished.

Motherfucker!

Callie was gone.

FOURTEEN

CALLIE

"**Y**OU LOOK BEAUTIFUL, CALLIE. As gorgeous as your sister," Elliot announced, leaning against the bar as I approached him.

"Oh, good. We aren't pretending anymore."

He smiled. "Yes. It did get rather tedious, didn't it?"

"Is that a rhetorical question?"

"Only if you want it to be." His gaze raked over me, missing nothing. "I must confess I wish we met under different circumstances."

"What kind?" I asked before ordering a glass of red wine. His presence unnerved me, but also pissed me off. This asshole knew what happened to my sister. He was the man who turned her over to a group of ruthless criminals.

The bartender handed my drink over, and I took a sip, always keeping Elliot within view. I didn't trust him.

"The kind where a certain DOLL Agency allowed me to book your services. I'm rather fond of blondes. They do have all the fun."

Disgusting pig. I wouldn't let him rile me up.

"Is that your game? To fuck your way into prison? Seems rather droll."

His hand tightened around the glass of bourbon he drank, but he never lost his cocky, aggressive smile. "You have a way with words, Callie."

"Why not tell me the truth? What do you hope to gain by speaking in innuendo? It's ignorant and tiresome."

The first hint that I ruffled his feathers surfaced. A sneer replaced his smile. "Maybe this is only a diversionary tactic."

Right. Like I was stupid and didn't figure it out.

I batted my eyelashes. "Oh, how silly of me. I never suspected a thing."

Yeah, I had the market on sarcastic bitch cornered.

Elliot moved closer, taking the seat next to me at the bar. We kept our voices low, but it didn't lessen the sting or animosity between us.

"Would you like to know how often I fucked your sister? Sadie never said no to me. No matter what I wanted." His hand lifted and caressed my bare shoulder. "If you want to see her again, maybe we could have a similar arrangement. I'd love to watch your face as you come. Such a passionate woman would be remarkable in bed, especially when I have her tied up and at my mercy."

How the hell did this man become the mayor of Henderson? How did he rise to the height of popularity? Did money buy every step on the ladder of his success?

"You're despicable."

"But I fuck even better."

"So that's it. You just want a new doll to play with."

He shrugged. "I can have any woman I want except for you. That's incredibly attractive, Callie."

"And it will never happen."

"Never say never, my dear. Everyone has a price. You just have to find it."

"That's what's wrong with you. No one has ever said no and meant it."

"Irrelevant."

Flustered, I downed the rest of my wine. "I would never consent."

"Ah, but I don't need that. Once a bargain is made, I fulfill it."

What the hell did he mean?

I stood, feeling slightly dizzy. Blinking, I stared at Elliot as the room began to spin. Just as I tipped over, he stood and caught me. One of his arms wrapped around my waist, hugging me against his side.

His head lowered, whispering intimately into my ear. "I will have you, Callie Withers. In my bed. On my cock. We just have a little detour first."

Shit.

I glanced at the empty glass of wine on the bar.

He didn't.

"Ah, yes. I knew you would watch me, but you never suspected the bartender. A delicious mistake, my dove."

His tongue peeked through his lips, licking the side of my neck as I struggled to keep my eyes open.

"I have a feeling you won't disappoint."

The crowded bar never noticed I didn't consent to Elliot's hands on my body or the way he ushered me from the bar, apologizing for my inebriated condition.

I wasn't drunk. He drugged me!

My vision blurred as I realized someone met us and helped me into a vehicle. My head lolled to the side as Elliot slid next to me. His hand gripped my inner thigh, rising upward, and snaked its way between my legs.

I felt him slide my panties aside, pushing a finger inside me.

A groan fell from his lips. He turned his head, his mouth on mine as he added another, slowly pumping them in and out.

I wanted to scream, to tell him to stop, but I couldn't.

"Fuck. I don't want to wait."

A dark laugh echoed from the front seat. "If you take her before completing the agreement with Undertaker, I've been told to blow your fucking brains all over this car."

Elliot withdrew his fingers, glaring at the driver. "Fine. I can be patient. I'll have all the time in the world once she's mine."

"True enough," he replied.

The horror of what awaited me sank in, and I began trembling, unable to stop. A cold shiver ghosted my frame, and remained there, refusing to relent.

Elliot sniffed his fingers and licked them, sucking my essence off the digits. "You will be worth every price I had to pay."

As my vision darkened, I knew I would pass out. Terrified, I didn't have any idea what would happen when I finally woke.

Please, Hawk. Find me. I need you.

HAWK

No. No. No.

This couldn't be happening.

Fuck!

I lifted a fist, punching it through the drywall with a roar, not giving a fuck that every officer in the club watched me lose my shit. "Sonofabitch!"

"While I understand what you're feelin' right now, Hawk, I'd appreciate it if you didn't tear up the fucking clubhouse." Crow dragged smoke from his cigarette into his mouth, slowly exhaling as he ticked his chin toward the table. "Sit."

How the fuck could he be so calm?

"Pres, this shit is fucking killin' me! It's my ol' lady—"

"No shit?" Cuckoo asked, interrupting.

I ignored him, continuing with my tirade. "I won't stand for this! Undertaker has crossed the line! We need—"

"Sit down, Hawk."

I couldn't. Too fucking keyed up, I didn't think I could do shit except ride out of here with my crow and hunt down Callie's location. Nothing else mattered.

"Pres, I don't think you—"

"Sit. The. Fuck. Down." Crow narrowed his eyes. "I'm the fucking president of this club. What I say fucking goes. Or do you have a problem with that, Hawk? Because we can discuss it right the fuck now, SAA."

Goddamn. "No," I replied, pulling out my chair to sit at his side. "Fuck. I'm all twisted up, pres."

"We can tell," Claw snickered.

I lifted my middle finger as he pursed his lips, smacking them in a kiss.

Fucker.

"I found our smoking gun, pres," Eagle Eye replied as Crow picked up the bottle of Jack in front of him and took a hard swallow. Didn't even bother to use the shot glass in front of him.

"Well, don't leave me hangin'."

"Elliot Goodman owns extensive property in the Las Vegas and Henderson area. He's been renting out commercial real estate to local businesses. Hold on." Eagle Eye typed a few keys, clicking away as he flipped the laptop around.

We all squinted at the screen.

"You see it?"

Nope. I bet not one of my brothers here did, either.

"Shit," Eagle Eye cursed. "How about you, pres?"

Crow scrubbed a hand down his face. "I had no idea coming back here would be such a goddamn train wreck. Do any of you fuckers know how to communicate? Christ. It's like a goddamn adult daycare around here." He tipped back the bottle and let the amber liquid coat his throat. "Just give it to me straight, Eagle Eye. We need the information to nail Undertaker and the fucking mayor to the cross and end this bullshit. I've waited too fucking long to avenge my pops. My patience is fucking gone."

Well, shit. Time to stop fucking around.

Eagle Eye nodded. "I feel you, pres. Been spending every free minute that I have on this shit. It's taken some digging, but I found a connection between Elliot, Undertaker, and the CEO of the DOLL Agency. They all have the same fake employee and address listed on their financial records."

"No shit?" Claw asked, shaking his head. "Stupid fuckers."

"What's the name and address?"

"The name doesn't matter. It's the location. The mayor's estate in Lake Las Vegas. All the money laundering can be traced back to that fake employee with an invalid social security number."

Crow pushed the bottle of Jack Daniels aside. "You sayin' he's got paystubs for this fake employee leading back to him and his home address? And this employee also works for Undertaker and the DOLL Agency?"

Woah. "How the fuck has no one caught this before now?"

"I'd like to know the same thing," Raven growled. "Bree was hurt because of this information."

Eagle Eye shrugged. "I can't tell you that. It's not easy to uncover this information. They covered their tracks. I'm better at this than most people and more thorough. Right now, there's an envelope containing proof of these records being delivered to every major newspaper in the Las Vegas area. By tomorrow night, the whole state of Nevada will know what Elliot Goodman has done. The Dirty Death MC and the DOLL Agency will also be implicated." He sat back, ticking his chin at Crow. "Told you I had this, pres."

"You sure the fuck did," he agreed.

"And you found all of this on your own?" Raven asked, arching a dark brow.

"Well," Eagle Eye rubbed the back of his neck. "I had a little help. An anonymous email from a concerned citizen."

"What concerned citizen?" Crow stared at him as he squirmed in his seat.

"I don't know. She sent me the idea to look deeper into the fake employee. I would have found it," he assured us, "but she made it possible sooner."

"She?" I crossed my arms over my chest. "The fuck, Eagle Eye?"

"It doesn't matter. The intel provided what we needed."

Crow gave a stiff nod. "You're right. I don't care about the source. What matters is we have what we need to move against the Dirty Death and Undertaker."

"We do, pres."

"You did good, Eagle Eye," I praised, "but this doesn't tell me where Elliot took Callie or if she's with the Dirty Death MC."

"No," Crow agreed, "but we're not gonna stop until we figure it out."

Caw...caw.

The throaty rattle of my crow sounded distressed outside. He sensed my agitation. Fucking up Undertaker and the DDMC was high on the list of the club's priorities. I didn't mind that.

But getting my woman back trumped the club's decision, and I sure hoped I wouldn't have to choose.

FIFTEEN

HAWK

"HEY, BROTHER. HOW YOU been?" Rael asked as he answered my call.

"Not good," I growled. Since Callie was taken, I'd been restless, agitated, and ready to punch anyone who stood too close.

"Fuck. Tell me what's happening."

"You remember Undertaker?"

Rael cursed. "Goddamn. Yeah, I do. What did that piece of shit do now? Did you find him?"

"No."

"Then he's fucking causing trouble like usual."

"Yeah, he sure is," I growled, thinking of Callie. Undertaker better not touch her. I'd let my crow rip him into a hundred fucking pieces and scatter them across the Nevada desert.

"He's working with the fucking mayor here in Henderson. I told you the shady shit going down, but it's gotten a lot more complicated. The mayor kidnapped my ol' lady."

"You have an ol' lady?" He sounded surprised.

I wasn't offended. That playboy rep had followed me around for a long while but that was in the past now.

"Yeah, I do."

"Shit," he cursed. "What do you need?"

Just like that, Rael had my back.

"I need to find her. The tracker on her phone is disabled. You think the Reapers are up for this?"

"Fuck yeah."

Relieved, I nodded. "That means a lot to me. Callie is everything."

"I feel you, man. It's the same with my Nylah and the twins."

Rael's ol' lady had twin boys a few months back. If he was protective over her before, it was nothing compared to now. He understood how I felt.

"Talk to Grim. Let me know what he says."

I heard him walking through the Crossroads, calling out for Grim. The phone went silent for a minute as I waited.

"Pres says we're good. He's givin' Crow a call."

Thank fuck.

I couldn't break my promise to Callie. I had to help her sister, and if the Reapers located Undertaker's clubhouse, they would find the woman I loved too.

"Thanks, brother."

"Hey, we'll find her. There's no place Undertaker can hide from my Reaper."

The Tonopah chapter of the Royal Bastards MC had a closely guarded secret. They reaped souls, and their connection to the demons gave them abilities even the crows could never form.

"Give me the details, so I know what we're working with."

I filled Rael in about all this shit that had gone down since we last met. "And that sums it up," I finished.

"I swear to fuck you attract more drama than I do."

"Yeah, yeah. Piss off."

A dark chuckle filtered through my phone. "We're ready. I'll be in touch."

The call ended, and I walked outside for a smoke, hoping it wouldn't be long before I heard from him.

I SHOVED CARRION INTO the wall, fucking livid that he did this. "You said she had to go to that meeting. You fucking said I had to accept it or place her in irreversible danger."

"I did," he replied calmly.

"She's fucking gone!" I roared. "Undertaker has her!"

"He won't harm Callie. She's not the one he wants."

My chest heaved as I shook my head. "Not fucking okay, Carrion. This isn't right."

He reached out, grasping onto my wrist. *"See."*

His eyes did that crazy shit where they fluttered, rolling to white as he swayed. Ever since he died and Falcon brought him back to life, Carrion had been strange. Odder than usual. He never touched anyone, and now I learned why.

145

His gift had grown potent, as well as his connection to his crow.

The room faded, and I stood inside a bedroom with feminine décor in white and gold shades. Soft sheer curtains draped the bed, held back by golden fleur-de-lis. Vanilla-scented white candles flickered in a gentle breeze, sweeping in from outside. Exotic plants stood on golden stands around the perimeter. Sliding glass doors opened wide and led to a balcony where I spotted my Callie.

I shouted her name, trying to run but couldn't move.

"You're only an observer," Carrion informed me.

"Fuck." I didn't like this at all.

I watched Callie and Sadie hug, happy to see their reunion.

"I've missed you!" Callie wouldn't let go of her sister. "Why haven't you contacted me? Wouldn't he let you?"

Sadie shook her head. "No. I've been his prisoner the entire time."

"What about Carson?"

Who the fuck was that? The FBI agent? Fuck. Yeah, that was his name. Carson Phillips.

"He's here. I'm afraid Undertaker hurt him."

The door opened, heavy footsteps revealing the president of the Devil's Murder. Undertaker's back filled my vision. The man towered above the women, over six and a half feet tall. A giant.

"I've brought you company," he grumbled, staring at Sadie.

I sensed his obsession and desire for her, not the least bit interested in Callie.

"Become my mate, and I'll let her stay."

"If I refuse?" Sadie asked, clutching Callie close.

"I don't know how my beast will react."

"This isn't what you told me!" I shouted, shoving at Carrion again. "He'll kill her!"

"No," Carrion replied. "Watch."

"I can't be what you want," Sadie replied. "No woman will ever be enough for you. This monster that you've become, it only takes, feeds, and destroys. Even if I say yes, you'll end up killing me."

Undertaker opened his mouth and howled. An inhuman cry that sent chills down my spine.

"You have to cut ties with him to bond to me."

"Nooooooo!"

Sadie released Callie, walking from the balcony to his side. Her hand lifted, caressing the side of his face. "There's no other way. Release my sister. She can't save either of us. Only you can make that choice."

His answering growl frightened Callie, and she shivered. Sadie simply backed away. The two girls moved toward one another, clasping hands.

"As you wish," he finally relented.

The room disappeared, and I stood inside the bar of the Roost, backing away from Carrion as he released my wrist.

"Told you. You're too fucking stubborn, Hawk."

I didn't give a fuck. "Tell me where to find Callie."

"Just ride, brother. Go! Now!"

Christ! I rushed toward the door, not hesitating to listen.

"Head north!"

Fucking hell. What kind of directions were those?

I jumped on my bike, started it up, and sped out of the parking lot. I shifted gears and increased speed so fast I felt the Harley tremble beneath me.

The heavy growl of several motorcycles reached my ears, and I glanced in my mirrors. Raven, Crow, Claw, Cuckoo, and Jay were all behind me.

Thank fuck.

I had a feeling I would need backup when I reached Callie.

Fifteen fucking hours had passed. Carrion fucking left that part out because he knew I would never allow Callie to leave for that long. Who knew what the fuck was happening to her? Did the fucking mayor hurt her? Or hand her over to Undertaker and the Dirty Death?

The agony of not knowing was tearing me up inside.

I rode all the way to Vegas, zipping down the strip and outside the city, still traveling north. There was no sign of Callie. I didn't know what the fuck to look for or what to do. If something happened to her, I wouldn't be able to control the crow. He'd fucking go feral.

Up ahead, I saw a row of motorcycles on the side of the highway. A dirt road led to the left, and I followed it, kicking up dust behind me as I sped toward the building in the distance. Nevada had several of these old warehouses in the middle of nowhere, way too fucking close to Area 51. People liked to imagine all kinds of crazy alien theories, but none of that mattered to me.

I rode hard, closing the distance until I spotted her outside. One of her wrists was cuffed, the other half of it looped to a chain that wrapped around a metal pole. She was fucking pissed, fighting off whoever stood next to her. With glee, I noticed the mayor trying to subdue my woman. His hand lifted, and he slapped her, knocking her head into the pole.

That was when I lost control of the crow.

He decided to combine our spirits, and his rage would be magnificent.

GALLIE

ELLIOT TOOK ADVANTAGE OF my weakened state and cuffed one hand, attaching it to the pole stuck in the ground. The chain rattled as I shook my arm, desperate to gain freedom.

"You sick son of a bitch! Let me go!"

I didn't have any memory of how we arrived here. After being drugged, I ended up at the Dirty Death MC compound. My reunion with Sadie was short-lived and frightening as the behemoth president of the club charged into the room he'd kept her prisoner in. I barely had a chance to speak with her before he hauled me outdoors, shoved me into Elliot's arms, and ordered him to deliver me to this address.

Elliot complained the entire time. He got stuck driving, which pissed him off, followed by the fact that I tried to escape several times. Now, here we were, yelling at one another in the middle of the desert.

I didn't know if Sadie was here or not. I hadn't seen her yet.

"Would you stop screaming at me? I can't handle all this fucking stress."

Seriously? What a pussy!

"You're ridiculous! I'm surprised you have a cock at all. Are you sure you don't use a strap-on to fuck women?"

He roared with fury, pulling back his arm. I knew it would hurt when he slapped me, but I didn't expect to be thrown backward, my head smacking into that stupid metal pole.

The chains rattled above my head as I slumped to the dirt.

"Fuck!" He shouted, pulling at his hair. "I didn't agree to this!"

"Too late now," I announced in a sing-song voice. "You reap what you sow."

"Shut up!"

Where was his confidence now? His control? I had never met a man as weak and pathetic.

Something rumbled the ground beneath our feet. At first, I thought it was an earthquake, but then I realized it was a dozen motorcycles, all heading in our direction.

At the front, leading the way, I spotted Hawk.

Finally. He found me.

I couldn't contain my smile. The side of my face burned from the slap, and the back of my head throbbed, but I wouldn't be lying in the dirt long. Hawk would save me.

I hoped he kicked Elliot's ass.

The mayor still had a few surprises left inside him, though, as he whipped out a gun, pointing it at my head. He stood there, watching Hawk slow down, braking before jumping off his bike. He didn't even put down the kickstand. Damn. My man was worried about me.

"Hey, handsome!" I yelled, my voice slightly slurred.

I guess the drugs were still in my system.

"Callie!" He shouted. "What the fuck did you do to her?" Hawk charged us, his body vibrating with fury.

I couldn't be sure, but I thought I caught his entire frame flicker, wobbling like water in clear glass. Blinking, I didn't understand what was happening. Did the drugs do something to my brain?

What happened next defied logic. It didn't make sense.

Black feathered wings sprouted from Hawk's back as he lifted a foot off the ground, flying toward our direction.

As he reached us, I noticed the feathers extended down his arms, covering his skin from shoulder to wrist. Beautiful, shiny onyx feathers. Such a pretty bird. Uh, man. His nails had grown into claws as he lowered to the ground, lifting his hands.

"Don't fucking fire that gun."

I stared at the biker who owned my heart.

A fucking lifesize crow. My man had changed into Hawk, like the fictional character from DC Comics, only he was way sexier. Low-slung jeans on his hips. Bare chest rippling with muscle. And a killer smile.

I think I just popped a lady boner.

Hawk resembled a dark angel, hell-bent on retribution as he stalked toward us.

Elliot pulled back the hammer on his weapon and cocked the gun, smiling at Hawk. He didn't seem surprised by his transformation. Was I just imagining it?

What kind of drugs did he dump in my drink?

Woozy, I blinked, resting my head against the pole.

"You okay, my goddess?"

"Never better," I replied, squinting at him through the bright sunshine. "Could use a hand."

"I've got you covered."

"I know."

His gaze refocused on Elliot. "You've been a pain in the ass for far too fucking long, Goodman."

Elliot's eyes narrowed. "I know what you are. You, your club. Undertaker and the Dirty Death. You think I'm scared? Fuck off. You don't have the balls to kill me." He turned to me, flashing a sinister grin. "Your pussy tasted good, Callie. I'm looking forward to stretching it out."

Oh, shit!

Hawk flew forward, slamming into Elliot. The gun discharged as I screamed, yanking on the cuffs.

Everything happened so fast.

Hawk and Elliot tumbled to the ground, rolling in the hot desert sand. Black feathers obscured my view. I couldn't tell if either of them were shot. Fists pounded, and limbs tangled as my vision narrowed. Dark spots danced in the corners.

Looking down, I noticed the wet spot seeping into the material of my cocktail dress. My gut burned as I groaned.

Did Elliot shoot me?

"Hawk?"

The word escaped my lips in time to notice three things. One, Elliot fell to the ground, his bloodied body showing no sign of life. Two, Hawk was limping. Three, my hand lifted, covered in bright red fluid.

I said the only thing that mattered.

"I love you, Hawk."

SIXTEEN

HAWK

CALLIE LOOKED FAR TOO pale. She lost too much blood after being shot in the abdomen. How ironic that she would gain a similar wound and scar to the one I received the day we met.

Fucking Elliot Goodman.

I hope he rots in hell.

The bastard shot my woman and then tripped, squeezing the trigger on his fucking gun, firing into his chest. He got off way too fucking easy. I should have let the crow rip him to pieces. I sure wanted to but couldn't do shit once I saw Callie had been shot.

I rushed her to the emergency room, but she never regained consciousness when we reached the hospital. They wheeled her away into surgery, and I never even fucking got to tell her that I loved her.

153

My heart felt heavy as I sank into the chair beside her bed, listening to the consistent beating of her heart on the monitor. For two days, she slept. Never once did she open her eyes.

The worst part? We never found Sadie. Or any hint about Agent Carson Phillips. Rael found the Dirty Death MC compound empty when the Reapers arrived. He said they'd try to track them down, but I knew the wolf left with his pack, Sadie, and the FBI agent.

Undertaker planned this. He wasn't at the warehouse, and it pissed me off we missed our chance to hunt him down. The fucker played us. He dropped Elliot Goodman into our lap to take the asshole down, but he was only a temporary fix to the main problem.

Undertaker still had to atone for Rook's death. The club wouldn't accept anything other than his death, and the crows wanted to be included in our revenge.

The television anchored to the wall in Callie's room flashed the latest headlines. For the last forty-eight hours, the media coverage of Mayor Elliot Goodman's corruption scrolled across the screen. Every social media outlet in the country posted about his criminal activities and connection to the missing women in the Las Vegas area. Most people seemed shocked about it, and I heard the hospital staff gossiping. The truth about his money laundering and theft hit the community hard. Outside City Hall in Henderson, protestors rioted. The shit had hit the proverbial fan.

Reaching for Callie's hand, I held it, lightly rubbing the skin with my thumb. I didn't care how long it took her to wake up, but I wasn't leaving until she did.

Claw sat across from me, playing cards on a folding table we brought with us. I didn't see the fun in Solitaire, but he seemed relaxed, so I didn't give him shit about it. Out of all my brothers, it surprised me that he was the one who remained here. I knew he had a dark past and hated hospitals.

"You don't have to stay, man."

"I don't mind."

"It's fucking boring."

"So? I'm not a toddler. I don't have to be entertained every minute of the fucking day."

Says the guy who's played with cards for the last five hours without stopping.

"Yeah, okay. Just makin' sure."

He smirked. "If you need a potty break or something, just let me know."

"Fucker."

He laughed, slapping more cards on the table.

The door opened, and a nurse entered. She glanced at us but stared at Claw for longer than seemed polite. Clearing her throat, she checked on the monitors.

"She's stable. You sure you don't want a snack or take a walk? I can keep an eye on her until you return," she offered.

"No. I'm good. Appreciate the offer, though."

"No problem." Her gaze drifted to Claw again. "What about you? Anything I can get for you?"

If that wasn't an open invitation, I didn't know what could be.

Claw lifted his head, sliding his gaze over her body with unhurried pleasure. I supposed she was pretty enough, but I wasn't interested. Claw rose to his feet. "Got a coffee machine?"

"Right this way."

I chuckled as they left, knowing he probably planned to fuck her in some supply closet. A month ago, I would have done it and not thought twice.

Funny how life could change in an instant.

A soft sigh caught my attention, and I turned, hope flashing through my body like a heatwave. I nearly teared up when Callie opened her eyes, murmuring my name.

"Baby, you're awake."

She frowned, blinking her eyes. "Thirsty."

I lifted the cup on her bedside table and brought the straw to her lips. She drank a few tiny sips, then rested her head against the pillow.

"You know I don't like to be called that."

"I know. It slipped out." Fuck. I couldn't stop smiling.

"What's the matter with you? You're grinning like a fool."

"I'm just happy to see you, sweetling. Missed those pretty gray eyes."

"Hawk."

"Renner," I corrected. "Well, Renner James, to be exact."

"Your real name?"

"Yep. I'd like to hear you say it the next time you're coming on my tongue."

A flush crept into her cheeks.

"You've been out for several days. Kinda worried me," I admitted.

She moved her hand to her stomach, remembering the gunshot wound. "Am I okay?"

"Yes."

"Can I still have babies?" Her eyes filled with tears, and my heart nearly shattered.

"I think so. I didn't ask because I didn't want to overstep."

"I want to know. Now."

Callie buzzed for the nurse's station. "Send in a doctor, please. I need to talk to someone about my chart."

The wait nearly killed me, but twenty minutes later, an older man in a white coat entered, greeting us. He had thick salt-and-pepper hair and a deep voice.

"How can I help you, Callie?"

"I was shot in the stomach. Can I still have children?"

The doctor blinked. "Well, yes."

"You're sure?"

"Absolutely."

"But how do you know it didn't damage any of my reproductive organs?"

The doc smiled. "Good question. Well, we did some X-rays. There's no internal bleeding. No trauma to any internal organs. You were lucky."

Callie nodded, relieved.

"But you do have something in your file you should know about."

Oh, shit.

"What is it?"

The doc looked unconcerned, but I felt like I would puke.

"You have nine months to figure it out."

He waited for the news to sink in.

"I'm pregnant?"

"Yes. So early, you wouldn't know yet, but we caught it. I'll add prenatal pills to your prescription list. Congratulations!"

He excused himself, leaving us in stunned silence.

Holy fuck. I knocked up Callie. And holy motherfucking fuck, I was going to be a father.

"Are you okay?" Callie asked, squeezing my hand. "Happy?"

Hell yeah. It might be too soon for some, but not us. Fate brought us together and wasn't letting us grow apart. I could accept that.

"I fucking love you, babe. This is amazing news."

I couldn't hold out any longer and leaned over, capturing those sweet lips I couldn't taste or kiss enough.

Yeah, I planned on making Callie my ol' lady as soon as she was discharged from the hospital.

And if she'd have me, I planned to marry her too.

CALLIE

"TAKE IT EASY, BABE. There's no rush." Hawk hovered as his hands settled on my waist, steadying me once we entered the Roost. The familiar leather and lemon scent filled me with a feeling I hadn't experienced since I was a kid. Home.

"I'm fine."

"Sweetling, you were shot in the stomach, kidnapped, and you're having my baby. This is nothing compared to how protective I'm feelin' right now."

"He's going to get worse," Raven joked. "Trust me. I'm the same way with Bree. Maybe worse."

My gaze shot to the inside of the bar, landing on Bree.

She shrugged. "Yeah. I'm preggers too."

"Oh my God!" I squealed, rushing toward her. "This is so awesome! Our babies will grow up together."

Her smile widened. "You're right! I love it."

Raven placed his hand over his heart, mouthing *I love you.*

She inhaled a deep breath and released it. "I'm so happy we're doing this together, Raven."

If I didn't know better, I would swear that big silver fox blinked back tears.

I hugged Bree, thrilled not to be doing this alone. "Congrats, bestie."

"Same to you, BFF."

We snickered as we separated.

Bree cleared her throat. "Did you find Sadie?"

Sighing, I nodded. "Yes, and lost her again."

"Oh no!"

I had to trust my sister. She asked me to give her time to sort out the complex triangle involving her, Undertaker, and Carson. The situation worried me, but I couldn't make her choices for her. Sadie was the orchestrator of her own happiness. Confused, I didn't understand the connection that formed between her and that monster Undertaker. Sadie never had a chance to elaborate other than she believed Undertaker held Carson prisoner. I just hoped she didn't plan to sacrifice herself for the FBI agent. Maybe Hawk and the Devil's Murder would find her before that occurred.

"We're on it," Hawk assured Bree. "The club won't rest until Sadie is safe."

I held out my hand, and he snaked his arm around me, dropping a kiss on my lips. I nearly melted into him.

His warm breath whispered into my ear. "You're tired."

Yawning, I rested my head against his shoulder.

"Let's go," he murmured into my ear. "You need rest."

I didn't argue. He was right.

The future may be unknown, but I had the devotion and protection of a man who would do anything for me and my sister in order to make our family whole.

That meant everything.

There were questions I wanted to ask, things I needed to learn about Hawk. I didn't understand how he could change into a crow, and right now, it didn't matter.

I knew I loved him. Fate could figure out the rest.

UNDERTAKER

THE RANCID, MILDEW-SATURATED odor of the underground cell burned my nose. I fucking hated dragging Sadie down here, but she refused to cooperate after I sent Callie away.

My hand wrapped around her upper arm, tucking her close against my side as we descended into the bowels of the prison my pack built a century ago for those who tried to hunt us down.

Nothing changed in all that time. Humans were skittish and easily frightened of the supernatural. They didn't understand we weren't a threat as long as they left us in peace.

Not true, I argued in my head. *Not when you let the vargulf loose.*

Snarling, I stomped through puddles of muck. I didn't want to listen to the argument. It didn't change a damn thing.

"Where are we going?"

"To finish this."

She was startled at my words. "Finish what?"

"The last connection I need to sever to claim you."

For the first time, she fought me. Her fists pummeled my chest as I picked her up, arriving at the cell where Agent Carson Phillips had resided for the last couple of months.

"Put her down!" he shouted when he saw who I held. "Please!"

"No," I huffed, clutching Sadie against me. My fingertips brushed her shoulder possessively.

She swatted them away with a frown. Her eyes widened when she took in the prisoner's dirty, disheveled appearance. "Carson? Oh my God!"

"Sadie!" He reached through the bars, desperate to touch my female.

"Don't touch my mate!" I roared, slamming a fist into the metal bars.

Carson stumbled, withdrawing his hands. His chest heaved as he shook his head. "I still don't know what you want from me."

"Her surrender."

Carson's features twisted into a snarl. "No!"

His pathetic cry did nothing to extend his life or change my mind. "Release her to me."

He blinked. "I don't know what you mean."

"You do," I contradicted. "You know why you're here. Sever your connection. Now."

Sadie's confused brown eyes watched the two of us. "I don't know what's happening."

Carson smiled, *fucking smiled* at the female I coveted. "You're worth it, Sadie. Every minute. Every sacrifice. All the love in my heart."

Her stricken expression pleased me. This would be over soon.

"I need you to trust me, my love. Will you do that?"

Sadie reached for the metal bars, but I yanked her hands away. She sent a glare in my direction. "I will always trust you, Carson."

"Good. Do something for me."

"Anything."

"I need you to run. Now!"

She darted toward the stairs as I swung my fist into the bars. Carson lifted his hands, chanting something I didn't understand. As soon as the words left his mouth, I stumbled to my knees.

No!

The ground shook as my vision tunneled, all the light disappearing in an instant. Nothing but eternal black remained. Blinded, I cursed and roared my fury, unable to control the shift that followed. My body began to contort, transforming into the monster determined to gain control.

The vargulf unleashed, and his fury would reach across the entire state of Nevada.

Fuck.

My head began to pound as ringing flooded my ears.

The last thought in my head, taking hold above all others, was the reality that I would kill my mate and her lover.

The carnage would be magnificent.

EPILOGUE

HAWK

Three months later—

"FUCK. YOU LOOK BEAUTIFUL." I practically salivated as I stared at the fierce, gorgeous goddess I planned to propose to on our date tonight. She didn't have a clue what I had planned. Staring at the slight rounding of her tummy, I smiled at the son growing in her womb. My son.

Fuck. I nearly preened as ridiculously as the crow.

Knowing I was about to bring a kid into this world both terrified me and excited me. A part of me believed I was too fucked up after the childhood I had. That fear wouldn't control me. The vile words spewed by the sperm donor who created me no longer influenced my life.

All that mattered now was the future and the woman I wanted to share it with. Us. Together.

And my club. The brothers I called family.

We had shit to deal with before we could fully heal.

But that wasn't what I wanted to concentrate on today.

I took Callie's hand, leading her to my bike. "I've got a surprise for you," I announced as I placed the helmet over her head, ensuring she rode safely.

The ride down Hwy 95 to our location didn't take long. We rode to Lake Tahoe and stopped at a place the club bought next to the lake. The house was a shared property big enough to host a few families for anyone who wanted to use it. I booked the weekend and parked on the driveway as we arrived, excited to share it with Callie.

"You're gonna love this place, sweetling. It's right on the lake."

Callie squeezed my hand as I led her up the steps of the porch and around the deck, only stopping once we reached the edge of the lake. Cool water rippled in the gentle breeze sweeping across the endless blue crystals dancing on the surface. The sun's rays shimmered over it as I lowered to one knee.

Callie gasped as I held her hand.

"I'm not a guy with fancy words. This is about the best I can do for ambiance."

She smiled. "It's pretty good, Hawk."

"I want you to be my ol' lady. The woman who wears my property of Hawk cut and stands by my side. It won't be easy, and club life isn't for everyone. I think you got what it takes to be a badass biker bitch, babe."

She laughed at that.

"I got you right here, babe." With my free hand, I tapped my chest over my heart before reaching inside my cut to pull out a tiny black box. "You're in my heart to stay. I fucking love you, Callie. You're my ride or die. Tell me you'll marry me, and we can ride this life together. Always."

Tears pooled in her gray eyes. "Oh, Renner."

Fuck. Hearing my real name made this fucking perfect.

"Is that a yes?"

"Will you turn into a crow again?"

"I don't know. Maybe. If he senses you need his protection, then yeah, I fucking will."

"Will you take me on rides on your Harley every week? And never leave our child and me?"

"Yes. This is forever, my goddess."

"Then, yes. I love you, Hawk. You make me so happy."

Yes!

I scooped her up into my arms, swinging her around as her laughter floated around us. My head lowered, and I captured her lips, deepening the kiss until she pulled away, panting for breath.

Caw...caw.

The crow approved. He dipped his chin, ruffled his feathers, and flew away. I knew he wouldn't go far.

The crow and his mate bonded for life.

And my love, protection, and devotion would last until my death.

Cradling Callie's face in my hand, I stared into her eyes, finding a completeness of soul I had always longed for.

Even a wild biker like me could be tamed. It just took the right woman.

I pulled out the engagement ring and slid the diamond onto her finger, grinning like a goddamn fool.

She swiped tears from her cheeks, gazing at me like I was her whole fucking world. The man she counted on. The guy who helped save her sister and rescued her from a vile predator. And soon, the father of her unborn child. So much love poured from her into me that I couldn't speak.

Some moments were too fucking perfect for words.

TALON

"FUCK," I CURSED, BOUNCING my leg as I waited for Crow's sister to exit the pharmacy where she worked. Her shift should have ended about ten minutes ago, and she usually left right on the dot.

For the last two months, I'd been watching over her as my pres asked. He didn't want us to interfere in her life. His pops had kept her a secret, and none of us knew why. Rook should have told his son if no one else, but he didn't.

He died with that knowledge.

But then an envelope arrived with his handwriting on it and documents with her name on them, and Crow had to know if she was alive. I didn't blame him. If I had any family left on this earth, I'd want to know they were safe.

Turned out Crow's sister, a raven-haired bombshell named Gail was thriving, fucking gorgeous, and living in Carson City. I hadn't left since my pres sent me here, and I couldn't lie to myself that the gig wasn't a good one. I got to spend my time stalking a sexy brunette, and I didn't have to do shit but ensure she got to where she was going each day safely.

Didn't hurt that she was easy on the eyes, either.

I stood outside for another half an hour, agitated as fuck, until she appeared. Her expression explained the delay. She'd had a rough day, and it showed.

Caw...caw.

I heard the crow as he landed on a nearby roof.

"Yeah, I don't like to see her so stressed or tired either," I muttered.

I tailed the SUV she drove to her house, parking down the street like I did every night. Jogging to her place, I crept among the shadows, watching her park in her garage. Thank fuck, there were plenty of trees and shrubberies to hide my big ass as I stalked her like this. Didn't need to spook her in the process.

I should have noticed something was off.

The crows landed on her roof, cawing like mad. Not just one. A whole fucking murder.

Shit!

When I heard her scream, all bets were off. I didn't care about my orders. If someone was hurting that sweet girl, I would make them pay.

Rushing inside the garage, I followed her into the house. My gaze bounced all over, finding the mess someone left behind. All the furniture was tipped over, and shit spilled everywhere.

She turned on me, frightened, when she saw the gun in my hand. A second scream left those pretty plump lips, and I cringed.

Fuck. I just screwed this up.

Crow was gonna be pissed.

There's much more to come with the Devil's Murder.

The next book in the series, **Talon**, will be released in late 2023, followed by Crow's Revenge in early 2024.

Sadie's story isn't over. In order to finish it, she needs to tell her truth. Watch for more in the Devil's Murder MC series.

You can read more about Grim and his club in the Royal Bastards MC Tonopah, NV Chapter, now available.

Find all Nikki's Royal Bastards MC and Devil's Murder MC books on Amazon and Kindle Unlimited.

Never miss out on a book! Follow Nikki on social media to receive updates.

Hawk

#1 Crow

#2 Raven

#3 Hawk

#4 Talon

#5 Crow's Revenge

#6 Claw

#7 Cuckoo

#8 Carrion

#9 TBD

Love motorcycle romance?

Check out these books by Nikki Landis:

Royal Bastards MC Tonopah, NV

#1 The Biker's Gift

#2 Bloody Mine

#3 Ridin' for Hell

#4 Devil's Ride

#5 Hell's Fury

#6 Grave Mistake

#7 Papa Noel

#8 The Biker's Wish

#9 Eternally Mine

#10 Twisted Devil

#11 Violent Bones

#12 Haunting Chaos

#13 Santa Biker

#14 Viciously Mine

#15 Jigsaw's Blayde

#16 Spook and Specter

#17 Infinitely Mine

#18 Grim Justice

#19 TBD

Royal Bastards MC Las Vegas, NV

#1 Hell on Wheels

#2 Reckless Mayhem

#3 Jeepers Creepers

#4 Rattlin' Bones

#5 TBD

Royal Bastards MC Crossover

Manic Mayhem

Twisted Iron

Ravage Riders MC

#1 Sins of the Father

#2 Sinners & Saints

#3 Sin's Betrayal

#4 Life of Sin

#5 TBD

Lords of Wrath MC

#1 Tarek

#2 TBD

Iron Renegades MC

#1 Roulette Run

#2 Jester's Ride

#3 TBD

Pres/Founder – Crow

VP/Founder – Raven

SGT at Arms – Hawk

Enforcer – Talon

Secretary – Carrion

Treasurer – Claw

Road Captain – Swift

Tail Gunner – Jay

Member/Tech – Eagle Eye

Member/Cleaner – Cuckoo

Member/Healer – Falcon

Prospect – Goose

Prospect – Robin

SNEAK PEEK

I BECAME A MURDERER by accident. There was no premeditation, no desire to snuff a man's life. At least, not before tonight. The body lying below my feet in a pool of his blood, still sticky and warm, deserved to be punished.

And I was happy to do it.

I slit his throat with one of my knives and watched the lifeblood leak between his fingers as he feverishly pressed his hands to his neck. As if he could prevent the reaper—or the phantom—from taking his pound of flesh. An eye for an eye. Justice.

Touch what belonged to me, and ruin would follow—preferably death.

Javier Barone should have suffered longer for attacking Bianca and terrifying her the way he did.

The piece of shit was an animal. There were two rape charges against him, and it sickened me that Alaric Huber allowed him on the property.

After I left the body, my anxiety skyrocketed, not for the dead man soaking into his blood, but for *Bianca mia.*

Everything happened so fast. I didn't get a chance to check on her and ensure she was alright. Pissed, my hands formed fists, only loosening when I found the slope of the roof and climbed my way back to the veranda.

She was crying. *Merda!*

Her suffering felt like my own. I grabbed at my chest, nearly stumbling into a wall. No. I had to make this better.

Getting this close was folly. I should have stayed away, but my heart wouldn't allow it. I dropped silently onto the veranda, approaching her with hands raised, moving slowly not to spook her. Tears glistened on her cheeks. Her big blue eyes, usually bright and clear, were cloudy and dull.

I couldn't resist picking up her hand and kissing the surface, inhaling the sweet aroma of her soft skin. "Don't cry," I grunted, "it pains me to see it."

She didn't get a chance to answer.

Screaming broke out below us, and I knew Javier's body had been found.

"An eye for an eye," I announced darkly, backing away to merge into the shadows where I belonged, not in the light where Bianca, *mio angelo*, could shine alone.

I waited long enough to catch the expression on her face, a mixture of confusion, concern, and, finally, satisfaction. Relief followed. No figure from her nightmares would harm her again.

Thinking of that slight smile of satisfaction on her face made my cock swell with need. While she was innocent, Bianca also had a wild, rebellious side.

She craved a little danger and didn't shy away from the macabre.

That sliver of darkness called to me, and I loved the fact that she enjoyed my little gift.

"From me to you," I whispered, returning to the shadows to observe *la mia bella bambola* at my leisure. A consistent guardian who followed in her wake, vigilant against further harm.

I wondered if someday she would ask my name and become curious about the demon of the night.

Would she, *could* she, see the man behind the monster? The one who would die to protect her, who championed and watched over her since the day we met?

I never hoped for anything, not since the day I learned monsters were real, and they took the form of people who enjoyed preying upon children.

But for this? Bianca? The chance to be seen for who I was inside and not the ruined man on the outside . . . I dared to hope.

Nearly an hour later, I found Bianca at the back of the estate.

Another fated moment destined to change the course of our lives.

The vision in white monopolized every cell in my brain while the blood in my veins surged, swelling and thickening my cock. She had no way of knowing how I reacted to her, how deeply rooted she'd become, taking residence in my head and heart. Dangerous, probably to us both.

I couldn't see the man who walked beside her through the gardens, illuminated only by the faint amber glow of the paper lanterns above their heads. With a frown, I decided to move closer, traveling in tandem on the opposite side of the hedges, which allowed perfect concealment.

The stranger's hand brushed across Bianca's shoulder, dipping far too close to her breast.

As if the exposed cleavage wasn't enough to piss me off, the man ogled her like a juicy fat steak he couldn't wait to devour.

Even though his touch upon her skin lasted only a couple of seconds, it felt like an eternity.

My gaze didn't leave the place where his hand touched until she pulled away, a slight blip of concern disappearing from her face as fast as it appeared. Ah, she didn't want his attention. *Good.*

Maybe I wouldn't have to kill him.

It was then that I noticed she'd taken the white rose I'd left for her and placed it in her hair. A virginal spot of white against the thick raven locks. I couldn't hide the grin that nearly split my face in two, even when it pulled too tightly on the left side of my face. Something stirred deep in my chest.

All I wanted to do was whisk her away and pull her into my domain, allowing her light to consume us both.

Without a worry, I continued to follow them through the maze of bushes and hedges, hoping she ended up alone. I craved another few minutes in her presence, just ten seconds of her sweet floral scent and those big sapphires staring up at me.

It wasn't meant to be.

"Will you be happy, Bianca?"

His question forced me to concentrate on their conversation.

"It doesn't appear that I have a choice."

What the hell did that mean?

"I've loved you since we were kids, *cara mia*. Surely you know that."

"Then why didn't you propose to me instead of forcing this engagement from my *nonno*?" Her eyes sparked with blue fire.

How the fuck did this happen without my knowledge?

Alaric Huber wanted his granddaughter to marry this fool. Why?

"Answer me, Rubio."

Rubio? My eyes narrowed into slits. I remembered his file. Rubio De Marco. A hired gun.

Bad news for *il mio dolce angelo*.

She wouldn't marry him, not as long as I had breath in my lungs. He wasn't getting anywhere near her after tonight.

Fury spiked in my veins, heavy and hot, as I nearly growled.

Staring at the man who dared to slip his arm around her, I finally took the time to assess his features. Realization dawned. He was the man from the theater. The one who stood next to Alaric after the performance, waving like a lunatic.

My brows pinched together.

I knew him. From where I wasn't sure, but I never forgot a face. Maybe the fact that mine had been ruined caused me to recall such details, but the man was familiar. He was connected to my past, and that couldn't be a coincidence.

Bianca purposely moved to let his hand fall away, and Rubio smirked. The fucker knew she didn't like his touch.

Every tolerant thought I had of him vanished. I took it all back, snarling with barely restrained rage.

He needed to die.

Rubio made his excuse, leaving Bianca to make her way back to the house alone. Glad he decided to fuck off and give Bianca a break, I followed behind her, leaving the shadows. It only took a few seconds for her to freeze, slowly pivoting on her foot to face me.

"I knew you were there."

I didn't answer.

"You heard, didn't you?"

Scowling, I nodded.

"I hate him."

What did he do to her to cause such a reaction?

"Tell me why," I growled.

"He forced himself on me five years ago."

What!?

How was that possible? I watched over her, protected her. The only unaccounted-for times occurred when she went away to school. Did he find her there? Hurt her?

"Were you harmed?"

She bit her lip. "No. I fought him off."

My neck cracked as I rolled my shoulders. "I won't let it happen again," I vowed.

"You can't stop it. I'm going to be his *wife*," she spat.

I lifted my hand, cursing as she turned around and walked away, her cute ass swishing with every step. She didn't get far before she bumped into one of the hedges and fell over, tipping onto the lawn.

A giggle fell from her pouty, kissable lips.

How did I miss that she'd drank too much?

"Benny," she whispered, rolling to her side. "Why did you abandon me?"

At first, I thought she spoke to me, but then I realized she didn't have a clue about my real identity. Then it hit me. She *missed* me.

Wow. I never stopped to think how deeply knowing her secret would impact me.

"*Angelo*," I whispered, crouching at her side. "You can't sleep out here."

She mumbled something unintelligible.

Scooping underneath her bottom, I lifted her, bringing her soft, curvy body into my frame.

The rightness of that moment nearly stole my breath.

She belonged with me. I could feel it.

The same way I knew five years ago that she'd changed my life forever the minute she walked into it.

I managed to sneak her into the house without detection, laying her on her bed and removing her shoes.

Staring down at her flawless, beautiful face, I swore I would find a way to release her from the engagement her grandfather forced her into, even if I had to kill Rubio De Marco to do it.

Manic Mayhem is available to read now!

SNEAK PEEK

I LEFT THE CHAPEL and headed straight for the guest room where Desi was staying. Shadow opened the door without a word as I approached, giving me a chin lift as I walked inside. Kid had suddenly become my first choice to protect Mimi, and it was a bit weird to admit that I wasn't pissed at him anymore.

"Katya misses you, Trixie. She's not doing well."

"I knew Katya was in trouble when she said she was pregnant. What did they do?"

Desi let out a sob, tucking her chin into her chest. "Sean beat her when he found out. He fucked her up, Trix. When she didn't miscarry, he said she would stay pregnant, and they would sell her baby once it was born."

Mimi paled, gasping as she shook her head. "No! That son of a bitch!"

Desi was crying hard, her shoulders shaking as she clenched her fists. "I hate him! He's the vilest human being I've ever met."

"No," Mimi disagreed, "Resnikov is worse."

Desi reached out as Mimi accepted her hug and the two women cried together, taking what little comfort they could in such a horrific situation.

"Sunshine?" I called out softly, my heart breaking for both women. "Can we talk?"

I might be a tough biker, but I wasn't that fucking cold.

Mimi immediately leaned back and rose to her feet, releasing Desi and swiping her small hands across her cheeks. "I'll come back later, Desi. Get some rest."

Desi nodded, laying back against the bed as her eyes fluttered and the dark circles beneath proved she was exhausted.

Mimi reached for my hand, and I took it, intertwining our fingers as we entered the hall, heading toward our room. It *was* ours. Everything I had belonged to her too. I wasn't so goddamn full of myself that I couldn't admit that Mimi was my woman and she could have whatever she wanted. We shared it all.

She sat on the bed when we entered, and I dropped beside her, still holding her hand to offer as much support as I could.

"I suppose you want to know about Sean Jones and Resnikov."

Nodding, I kept quiet, letting her take as much time as she needed to gather her thoughts.

"Sean Jones is a sadistic prick. He likes to rape the girls and keep them guessing which one is next. Solonik liked to choke girls as he fucked them. Alexi liked to beat them. Sean is twisted. He likes to take their ass as they're being raped and prefers to be the first one who violates every girl that comes in."

My jaw clicked in anger, and I held back my Reaper, realizing that was the one thing I hadn't revealed yet to Mimi. The final part of who I was before she could accept me for the man that would become her protector and vindicator. It was sure to be shocking when she found out. My body vibrated with rage, but I held myself in check, squeezing her hand lightly as she kept talking.

"Mikhail Resnikov is on a whole different level of evil. To put it into perspective, he sold his own niece into slavery. Katya is his family. His sister's daughter. He's as ruthless as they come. He stood there when Katya was flown into the U.S. and thought she was here for a modeling contract, watching as she was pushed down to the ground and Sean Jones raped her for over an hour."

Mimi's voice cut off as she swallowed hard, and my chest heaved, hating this motherfucker with every ounce of breath in my body.

"And what did he do to you?" I asked softly, hating the question and needing to know at the same time.

"What didn't he do? You know what Alexi did to me. I was kept chained to his bed on numerous occasions when I wasn't sucking dick or being used. Sean liked to share me with him. The two of them together," she paused, gritting her teeth, "was almost too much."

"I'm sorry," I blurted out, tugging her onto my lap as I held her as tightly as I dared.

"I would bleed afterward, and they didn't care, Dale. Resnikov would laugh as he stood by the door, jerking off as I screamed and cried for them to stop. Any reaction only made it worse. I learned to keep quiet, and it was usually over faster."

"Did they know about the Royal Bastards MC?"

"No, not to my knowledge. That must have changed after you saved me." She sniffled, cradling my face as our eyes met. "I never did say thank you. I don't know what would have happened, but I can't help but feel that you did more than save my life. You gave me a fresh start and a place to heal. You've been my friend and my hope, my anchor, and my lifeline. Without you, I wouldn't be whole again."

Her words sparked a fire inside me, and I wanted to lay her back against the bed and make love to her, worship her body, and prove to her that sex could be fantastic. A mutual satisfaction for both partners. My lips met hers in the softest of kisses, pressing with enough pressure and passion that she didn't doubt how I felt, but not enough to overwhelm her. When we separated, I brushed my thumb across her cheek in a gentle caress.

"It means a lot to me that you opened up like that, Mimi."

"We both know it needed to happen."

"Yes, and I should reciprocate."

Her arms slipped around my neck as I held her in my lap, holding her as close as I could.

"Blackjack was the name of the mission op we chose. Intel provided the location of known terrorists in a tiny town on the outskirts of Afghanistan. My team included some of the best Marines I had the privilege of serving with. Guys I had known for years. Some of them I met in boot camp."

"You were close," she responded, understanding.

"Yes. We dropped down in the middle of the night in all our gear, moving in nice and slow as we cleared each area slowly to ensure we didn't tip off the terrorists. We made it all the way to the house we suspected they were hiding in."

She bit her lip, sensing the rest of the story didn't have a happy ending, and she was right.

"We forced our way in, and that's when shit went crazy. My team got separated as we took on fire and fought back, closing in on the two leaders we were supposed to capture if possible but kill if necessary. The last room I moved into should have been empty. We cleared it, but somehow more of their soldiers moved in behind us."

"Oh no," she whispered.

"There was an explosion on two sides of the room. I watched as my best friend blew apart in front of my eyes." With the memory, my own eyes slammed shut. "I can still see the smoke and debris, smell the gunpowder and metallic tang of blood. It's like I never left sometimes. The cries of my brothers and the heavy gunfire mix together in my head. I remember the excruciating pain in my back, and I knew I was hit. All I kept thinking was that I hoped we got all of those motherfuckers and that I died with my fellow Marines."

"Dale," Mimi cried as I opened my eyes again, staring into the liquid pools of sky blue that were swimming in tears. "I'm so sorry."

"I've been lost since that deployment. Never could find my footing or stop having those goddamn nightmares."

"Everything changed when we met. You helped save me too, sunshine."

She lifted her hands and showed me her wrists. "See these scars? I tried to take my life one night after Sean and Alexi used me for nearly five hours. I was in so much pain that I could hardly breathe, and I just wanted it all to end."

My fingers rubbed over the scars, and I lifted each wrist, placing a kiss on the top. "We're good together, Mimi. Me and you, we get one another."

"We do, Patriot. That's something I've never had until now. You make me feel safe and wanted. It means everything."

My forehead lowered to hers, and we breathed together, letting the sorrow and pain of the past drift a little farther away.

"We're gonna make it, sunshine."

"When you say that, I actually believe you."

I kissed her one more time, leaning back to stare at the woman I was positive that I loved. It wasn't the right time to say those three life-changing words, but I would tell her soon.

Right now, I wanted to hold her a little longer and keep the monsters that wanted to tear us apart from closing in.

Hell's Fury is available to read now!

ABOUT THE AUTHOR

Nikki Landis is the USA Today Bestselling & Multi-Award-Winning Author of wickedly fierce romance. Her books feature dirty talkin' bikers, deadly reapers, dark alpha heroes, protective shifters, and seductive vampires, along with the feisty, independent women they love. There's heart-throbbing action on every page. Within her books, you can find suspense, fated mates, instalove, and soul bonds deep enough to fulfill every desire. Like your books on the darker side with plenty of spice? Look no further! Nikki also writes monster and sci-fi romance under the pen name Synna Star.

She lives in Ohio with her husband, boys, and a little Yorkie who really runs the whole house.

Made in the USA
Las Vegas, NV
30 June 2023

74091350R00120